THE
SACRED
MAYA
SMOKING SHELL

THE
SACRED
MAYA
SMOKING SHELL

A NOVEL

MANUEL M NOVELO

iUniverse, Inc.
Bloomington

THE SACRED MAYA SMOKING SHELL

iUniverse books may be ordered through booksellers or by contacting:

iUniverse
1663 Liberty Drive
Bloomington, IN 47403
www.iuniverse.com
1-800-Authors (1-800-288-4677)

ISBN: 978-1-4697-9074-9 (sc)
ISBN: 978-1-4697-9075-6 (ebk)

Printed in the United States of America

iUniverse rev. date: 03/09/2012

CONTENTS

The Northern Territories: People Of The Cloud
Serpent Clan

Altun—Ha the Hurricane Twenty Years Before

Nohoch Pek And His Band Of Renegades

The Sacred Jaguar

City Of The Far North: The Cloud Serpent Clan

The Caves: "Xibalba"

—Xibalba—

Dedication And Acknowledgment

I WOULD LIKE TO EXPRESS MY GRATITUDE TO MR. JOHN HART (LIBRARIAN) WHO TOOK TIME TO READ MY MANUSCRIPT. A HEARTFELT THANKS TO HIM FOR HIS SUPPORT ENCOURAGING WORDS AND ADVICE ABOUT THIS BOOK. THANK YOU JOHN.

TO MY WONDERFUL WIFE ELSY AND CHILDREN CHRISTY, BECKY AND ABNER WHO ALWAYS BELIEVED THAT I COULD MAKE THIS BOOK A REALITY. FOR ALL YOUR ENCOURAGEMENT I THANK YOU AND I LOVE YOU.

M.M.NOVELO

PREFACE

THE ANCIENT MAYA CIVILIZATION WAS ONE OF THE GREATEST THE WORLD EVER SAW. FROM ABOUT 250 TO 900 A.D. THEY LIVED IN THE GOLDEN ERA THE "CLASSIC PERIOD" OF THEIR WONDERFUL YET MYSTERIOUS CIVILIZATION. BY 900 A.D. AND BEYOND, FOR REASONS YET NOT CLEAR TO MAYA SCHOLARS AND LAYMEN ALIKE, THEY ABANDONED THEIR GREAT CITIES, SOME BUILDINGS STILL UNDER CONSTRUCTION, ONLY TO BE SHROUDED IN JUNGLE. THE ANCIENT MAYA WORLD ONCE COVERED PARTS OF SOUTHERN MEXICO, BELIZE, GUATEMALA, HONDURAS AND EL SALVADOR. THAT REGION TODAY IS STILL IS STILL REFFERED TO AS, THE MAYA WORLD, BY MAYA SCHOLARS, EPIGRAPHERS, AND ARCHEOLOGISTS.

MASONS, ARTISTS, AND SCULPTORS CREATED SUPERLATIVE WORKS OF ART IN THEIR HUGE CITIES. ARCHITECTS AND ENGINEERS

DESIGNED AND CONSTRUCTED MONUMENTAL BUILDINGS, BRIDGES AND CAUSEWAYS. THE MAYA HIGH PRIESTS HAD A VAST KNOWLEDGE OF ASTROLOGY AND ASTRONOMY. THEY COULD PREDICT ECLIPSES, PLOT THE CYCLE OF THE MOON AND THE PLANETS VENUS AND MARS WITH GREAT ACCURACY. THEY CREATED A HIGHLY ACCURATE CALENDAR NEARLY AS PERFECT AS TODAYS GREGORIAN CALENDAR. THE MERCHANTS ESTABLISHED THRIVING TRADE ROUTES BY LAND, RIVERS AND SEA. THEIR HISTORIANS AND SCRIBES COULD TRACE BACK THEIR ANCESTORS AND ROYAL LINEAGE FOR HUNDREDS OF YEARS.

THEY HAD A WRITTEN LANGUAGE AND A SYSTEM OF MATHEMATICS. THEY WERE ALSO ONE OF THE FIRST TO USE THE CONCEPT OF ZERO FOR MATHEMATICAL CALCULATIONS IN ASTRONOMY. TALENTED AND DEDICATED FARMERS PREPARED AND CULTIVATED THE LAND. A POWERFUL ELITE CLASS RULED THEIR HUGE CITIES AND GREAT ARMIES OF HIGHLY TRAINED WARRIORS PROTECTED THEIR CITIES AND PEOPLE. ABOVE ALL, THOUGH, THEY WERE ALSO GREAT ATHLETES AND THE ELITES AND PEASANTS ALIKE HAD A GREAT PASSION FOR SPORTS. PARTICULARLY FOR "POK-A-TOK" THEIR SACRED BALLGAME.

THIS IS A STORY OF THE GREAT MAYA CITY OF LAMANAI, [*CIRCA 650 A. D.*] *ITS RUINS ARE LOCATED* IN PRESENT DAY ORANGE WALK, BELIZE. A STORY ITS RULER WHO WAS DETERMINED TO HELP DEFEND ITS SISTER CITY CHAC'TEMAL FROM INVADING ARMIES OF THE CITIES OF THE FAR NORTH AT ALL COSTS NECESSARY.

ALSO, OF A YOUNG PEASANT BOY WHOSE NAME WAS BOX BALAM. HE WAS BORN AND RAISED IN THE MAGNIFICENT MAYA CITY OF LAMANAI ON THE WEST BANKS OF A BEAUTIFUL LAGOON. BY THE AGE OF FOURTEEN, HE HAD HIS MIND WELL MADE UP. HE WOULD BECOME A MEMBER OF THE FAMOUS AND WIDELY LOVED LAMANAI'S ROYAL POK-A-TOK TEAM [BALLGAME]. NOTHING OR NOBODY WOULD STOP HIM . . . .

AFTER THE SACRED CEREMONY THAT INITIATED HIM INTO MANHOOD TO BETTER PREPARE HIM IN BECOMING A SOLDIER AND A MEMBER OF LAMANAI'S ROYAL BALL TEAM, HE

WAS SENT ON A MISSION THAT ALMOST CAUSED HIM HIS LIFE . . . .

HIS FRIENDS AND HIS MENTOR WERE KILLED IN AN AMBUSH ATTACK BY SPIES OF THE FAR NORTH CITIES, NEAR LAMANAI'S SISTER CITY OF ALTUN-HA; HE HAD BEEN SEVERELY WOUNDED AND HAD FLED INTO THE INHOSPITABLE AND DANGEROUS RAIN FOREST. HE WAS VERY DETERMINED, THOUGH, TO SURVIVE AND RETURN TO HIS BELOVED CITY OF LAMANAI, HIS PEOPLE, AND THE GIRL HE FELL IN LOVE WITH. HE WAS ALSO DETERMINED TO STAY ALIVE SO HE COULD LATER FIND AND KILL THE PEOPLE RESPONSIBLE FOR HIS FRIENDS AND MENTOR'S DEATH.

AFTER WANDERING THROUGH THE JUNGLE INJURED, SICK, AND WEAK FOR MANY DAYS, SURVIVING ON WILD FRUIT, HE CAME ACROSS TWO MEN WHO . . . .

A STORY OF ADVENTURE, WAR, COURAGE, TREACHERY, LOVE, AND RISE TO GREATNESS IN AN ANCIENT CIVILIZATION.

EVEN THOUGH THIS IS A STORY OF FICTION ALL OF THE MAYA CITIES MENTIONED IN THIS BOOK ARE REAL. SOME OF THEM LIKE ALTUN HA, LAMANAI AND CARACOL HAVE BEEN PARTIALLY EXCAVATED AND RESTORED. SOME OF THEM STILL LAY COMPLETELY BURIED BENEATH THE JUNGLE OR RAINFORESTS OF **BELIZE** AND MIDDLE AMERICA. OTHERS LIKE HOLPATIN, IS BELIEVED TO BE BURIED BENEATH THE MODERN TOWN OF ORANGE WALK IN BELIZE WHILE PARTS OF THE ANCIENT CITY OF NOH MUL STILL LAYS BURIED UNDER THE SUGARCANE PLANTATIONS OF **NORTHERN BELIZE**.

MANY OF THE CITY NAMES ARE NAMES GIVEN TO THEM BY THE ARCHEOLOGISTS THAT EXCAVATED AND RESTORED THEM BUT MOST SCHOLARS AGREE THAT LAMANAI WAS THE ORIGINAL NAME OF THAT CITY. MOST OF THE ANCIENT TRADITIONS AND CUSTOMS MENTIONED IN THIS BOOK ARE ALSO REAL. AS MENTIONED IN BOOKS BY DEDICATED MAYA

Manuel M Novelo

SCHOLARS LIKE CHARLES GALLENKAMP, DR. DAVID PENDERGHAST, MICHAEL COE AND OTHER GREAT EPIGRAPHERS AND SCHOLARS. SOME OF THE ANCIENT MAYAN TRADITIONS MENTIONED IN THIS BOOK ARE STILL BEING PRACTICED TODAY BY SOME OF THE SURVIVING MAYA OF THE MAYA WORLD.

THE PEOPLE IN THE STORY

IN ALPHABETICAL ORDER

BIG TAPIR—Jaguar Order of Soldiers warrior chief. Brother of Box.

BOX BALAM—[Bosh Balam] Black Jaguar. Aspiring soldier and ball player.

CHACBE—War Captain and veteran soldier. Mentor to Box and Red Cat.

CLOUDS WINDOW CLAN—Clan of Box Balam, his family, and relatives.

CROCODILE TOOTH—Retired warrior chief of the Jaguar Order of Soldiers. Box's uncle.

EK BALAM—Sister of Box.

IXCHEL QUETZAL—[Ishel Ketzal] Ek's best friend and Box's fiancée

JAGUAR ORDER CLAN—Clan of the Royal Family of the city and provinces of Lamanai.

KANTUK—Honey Bee farmer. The vagabond.

LADY TZUK—Mother of Box.

LORD CHOC CHEN—Ruler of the city of Altun-Ha.

LORD GREAT MACAW—Son and successor to Great Mot Mot.

LORD GREAT MOT MOT—Ruler of the city of Chac' temal

LORD NOHOCH ZAK MAI—Ruler of the city of Lamanai and its provinces.

LORD SAC PEK—High Priest of Lamanai. Astronomer and prophet.

LORD TEPOCOATLE—[Tepokwatle] Ruler of one of the Far North cities.

RED CAT—Box's soldier friend and companion.

RED CLOUD—Wicked brother of Great Mot Mot.

SHINING BLUE STAR—Princess of Lamanai. Daughter of Lord Nohoch Zak Mai.

SILENT CAT—Father of Red Cat. Talented farmer of Lamanai.

THE CLOUD SERPENT CLAN—Clan of Lord Tepocoatle.

ZAK CHEN—Prince of Altun-Ha. Murdered son of Lord Choc Chen.

Places In The Story

IN ALPHABETICAL ORDER

ALTUN-HA—Stone Waters. Maya city in Central modern day Belize.

CAHAL-PECH—Place of Ticks. Maya city in Western Belize.

CARACOL—Sea Shell. Maya city in Western Belize.

CERROS—Hills. Maya city in the Corozal bay, Northern Belize.

CHAC'TEMAL—Red Lands, Believed to be present day Santa Rita in Corozal,Belize.

COPAN—Little Bridge. Maya city in Northwestern Honduras.

DZULUINICOB—[Zulwinicob] The New River in Orange Walk, Belize. River of Foreigners. A province that extended from Chac'temal to the Sibun River in Central Belize.

HOLPATIN—Land of the Canoe People. Maya city believed to be in present day Orange Walk Town and the surrounding area in Belize.

LAMANAI—Submerged Crocodile. Maya city in Northern Orange Walk District, Belize.

NOH-MUL—Big Hills. Maya city in Southern Orange Walk District, Belize.

PIEDRAS-NEGRAS—Black Stones. Maya city in North-western Guatemala.

THE FAR NORTH CITIES—Ancient cities of Central Mexico

THE GREAT OPEN WATERS—The Caribbean Sea

TIKAL—By, or at the Reservoir. Maya city in Northeastern Guatemala.

UAXACTUN—(Washactun] Eight Rocks. Maya city in Eastern Guatemala.

XUNANTUNICH—[Shunantunich] Maiden of the Rock. Maya city in the Cayo District, Western Belize.

OTHERS

IN ALPHABETICAL ORDER

ATLATL—A spear thrower. Adopted Maya war weapon

BALCHE—Intoxicating drink made from the bark of the Balche tree fermented with honey. Used in rituals, ceremonies, and celebrations.

CHULTUN—Bottle shaped underground reservoir.

COHUNE—Palm tree with clusters of edible nuts.

COPAL—Incense—aromatic resin from the Copal Tree.

CRABOO—Exotic yellow edible berries.

HAWACTE—An exotic fruit with edible nut inside the seed.

HUNAB KU—The supreme god of writing and wisdom.

IXCHELL—[Ishell] Goddess of childbirth, medicine and weaving.

JADE—A green stone found in the Motagua valley of Guatemala used for making jewelry.

KINICH AHAU—The sun god.

LUUM MAK—Ceremony marking the beginning of manhood for young Maya boys.

MAQUAHUILL—War club studded with obsidian or other stones.

MEKAPAL—Weight carrying bag with a long strap that can be attached to a person's forehead while resting the load on his back.

MILPA— A farm, a plantation.

NACOM—A Maya war captain.

OBSIDIAN—A glass like volcanic rock.

POK-A-TOK—Ball game of the Maya People.

Popol—Vuh—The Sacred Book of the ancient Maya that relates the creation of the Maya Cosmos and Maya People.

RAMON NUT—Bread Nut tree. A protein rich nut or seed that grows on huge trees found abundantly in the rainforest that requires no specialized cultivation. Roasted and ground in a flour to make porridge and other foods.

SACBEOB—White roads. Roads made with a gleaming white compact soil.

TAC'TE—Sacred ceremony for young Maya girls coming of puberty age.

TATA DUENDE—A mythological dwarf living in the rain forest with evil magical powers.

XBALANQUE AND HUNAPUH—[Shbalanke and Hoonapoo] Mythological Hero Twins and Pok-A-Tok players of the sacred Book of the ancient Maya people.

XIBALBA—[Shibalba] Caves believed to be portals of the underworld. Domain of demons.

XTABAI—[Shtabay] Mythological long haired maiden that lures young handsome men to their death.

ZAPOTE—A sweet edible exotic fruit.

CHAPTER ONE .

(THE CITY OF LAMANAI—CIRCA 650 A.D.)

For Box Balam, waking up this morning was glorious and wonderful. Every sound that came from the rainforest near his house was deliciously soothing and relaxing. The singing of the morning *Chacte* birds, the low guttural call of the colorful Keel Billed Toucan, the noisy chirping of the *Chachalacas*, the crickets in the nearby lawns and even the howling of the dominant male Black Howler monkeys as they were disturbed, probably by a passing Margay or other small wildcat, was sweet music to Box's ears. As a matter of fact, even the usually annoying call of the Cicadas, which he really detested sometimes, didn't bother him at all this beautiful morning. The call of the wild jungle animals sounded especially wonderful for young Box Balam on this day he awaited and dreamt about for so long. Far, far away deep in the jungle he thought he could also hear the roar of a mighty Sacred Jaguar.

As he looked through his window, Box could see a light drizzle falling through the rays of the almighty sun god Kinich-Ahau. The morning air was warm and thick already with humidity. Thus begun another day in the beautiful and great Maya city of Lamanai situated on the west banks of the mighty Dzuluinicob lagoon. The birthplace of and where the great, Dzuluinicob River, which unlike all other rivers in the region that ran from West to East, flowed South to North emptying into the great open sea into the bay of Chac'temal. The city of Lamanai had been named after the thriving crocodile population it had living in the river and lagoon. The crocodile was considered a sacred animal by the people of the Lamanai region. The great river was a very important trading route for the merchants of the city of Lamanai and other cities in the region. There were also other Maya cities like Holpatin and Noh Mul along the great Dzuluinicob River which were important trading cities for the Lamanai merchants. At the mouth of the great river where it emptied into the great sea were the Maya Cities of Chac'temal and Cerros Box Balam was a young and athletic Maya peasant boy who for months had dreamt about the coming of this day, the day of the Luum Mak ceremonies. In his excitement he had slept only a few hours the night before. He knew he should have gone straight to sleep, he would be needing all of his strength and energy on this day, but the excitement of being fourteen years old the next day had kept him awake. Just by thinking about what would occur today and all the festivities the different clans had prepared, and how it would change his life forever, filled his body and soul with energy and the desire to run, jump, and shout in happiness. But that time of the day had not yet arrived. Today was Box Balam's birthday, today he became fourteen years old. Box's fourteenth birthday had fallen on the exact day of the sacred Luum Mak ceremonies and this made him very happy. If the Luum Mak ceremonies had fallen a week or even two days before his fourteenth birthday then he would not had been included in Sacred Ceremony until the following year. He considered himself blessed and very lucky for that. The fourteenth birthday was a very important age for the boys of the Maya People. This was the age when, traditionally, the High Priests of the Jaguar Clan of the city of Lamanai officially declared the boys worthy in becoming a man. A holy ceremony was held every year to honor all the boys who had reached this age, elites and peasants alike.

After the ceremony, a huge traditional festivity was always held. It was declared a national holiday and everybody was expected to attend the ceremonies and festivities. The farmers, the masons, the painters, fishermen, the elites, the peasants, everybody took a day off from work on that special day in order to celebrate the coming of the Sacred *Luum Mak* ceremonies. At exactly five in the morning a warrior chief had blown a huge pink Conch Shell Horn while standing on top of the tallest Sacred Temple of Lamanai. He blew the great horn on the four directions of the cardinal points as it had traditionally been done for hundreds of years on this day and other special occasions. People could hear the horn blowing in villages miles away and they understood what it meant by its special sound. It was the signal for the people of Lamanai to begin preparing for the sacred *Luum Mak* ceremony and festivities. This special Sacred Conch Shell was only blown on very special occasions. Some of the older people remember it also being blown when the city was in danger of being attacked by the armies of the Cities of Far

North. That was a very long time ago, though, because for many years now there had been peace between the Maya People and the clans of the Far North.

This beautiful Sacred Conch Shell which was inlaid with shiny green Jade and sparkling Mother of Pearl and had a beautiful white and pink color, has been the sacred prized possession of the Royal Family of Lamanai for hundreds of years. The history books state, that hundreds of years ago this conch shell was brought to Lamanai by a young warrior prince from Holpatin. It had been presented to him as a gift by the ruler of the provinces of Altun Ha after a successful battle against foreign armies that had intended to invade the easternmost Sacred City and ceremonial center of Altun Ha, a sister city of Lamanai and Holpatin. The young prince had led the warriors that had successfully driven back the invaders and fierce warriors from the Far North.

On a trading mission to Lamanai the young prince, White Jaguar, had fallen in love and had married a young princess from Lamanai and had presented the beautiful conch shell to her. One of his grandsons later became ruler of Lamanai and was the great, great grandfather of the present ruler Lord Nohoch Zak Mai. It had ever since been used on very special occasions including to begin the sacred ceremony of the *Luum Mak*. It was kept in a small polychrome box inlaid with the most beautiful shiny green Jade in a room atop the highest Sacred Temple of Lamanai.

Hours before the Conch Shell Horn sounded, the women of the Lamanai clans were already hard at work preparing the food for the festivities. They also prepared many types of fruit juices and wines including Balche wine, an intoxicating drink reserved only for the men and the men to be. By seven in the morning the Sacred Plaza in front of the Sacred Temple which was adjacent to the Royal Palace, was already filled with people working. On the east side of the Royal Palace was the main plaza and people were also preparing it for the festivities.

Some of the men were busy building *ramadas,* which were thatched roof shelters, around the plazas to protect the visitors from the scorching Sun. They were using the leaves of the Cohune Palm tree, which could grow as long as thirty-three feet. The local musicians were already setting up in one corner of the plaza while the musicians that were invited guests to Lamanai from Altun Ha were setting up their instruments in a round wooden thatched kiosk in the middle of the plaza. Some of the musicians were blowing their flutes and horns making sure it sounded just right when the appropriate time came for them to start playing. Other musicians were tightening the skins on their drums while others were banging on them trying to get the right sound on it. Other musical instruments like Rattles, Turtle Shell percussions, Wooden Trumpets, Flutes, Conch Shell Trumpets and Rain Sticks were sitting on racks ready to start making sweet music.

Many other musicians and performers were invited from far away big cities like Caracol and Cahal Pech which were about three and two days journey Southwest of Lamanai, respectively. Itinerant performers and musicians also made their way towards the City of Lamanai on that particular day of the year. The sacred ceremony of *Luum Mak* was scheduled to begin at exactly midday as per tradition. That was when the great Kinich Ahau was shining directly and everywhere upon Lamanai. Decorators were placing beautiful colorful, aromatic flowers everywhere around the Sacred Plaza and on the stairways leading to the balcony atop the Sacred Temple where the ruler Nohoch Zak Mai and the High Priest would be seated during the ceremony. The balcony itself was decorated with beautiful wild orchids of innumerable bright colors. On each corner of the balcony were bunches of Black Orchids growing on pieces of logs. These were the princess' and the queen's favorite flowers by far. On each step were incensories filled with burning Copal Resin and its unmistakable sweet aroma hung everywhere around the plaza. Flanking the main front stairway, that led to the terrace of the Royal Palace, on the other side of the plaza, were twelve stucco masks, the images of past rulers of Lamanai. At the top of the steep stairway were two huge stucco masks on each side, the image of the present ruler Lord Nohoch Zak Mai and of his dead father. On the East wall of the palace strategically set, so that everyone could see it, was a huge Emblem Glyph of the city of Lamanai. Carved beside it was an equally large Long Count calendar.

On one side of the balcony was a cage with a beautiful young female Jaguar, the representation of the Royal Jaguar Order Clan. This was the ruler of Lamanai's very own clan that could be traced back for hundreds of years. Along the back wall near the Corbelled Arch door that led to the inside of the temple and then to a stairway that led to the Sacred Shrine on top of the temple, were cages of beautiful colorful birds like the Keel Billed Toucan, talkative Yellow and White Head Parrots, Scarlet Macaws, beautiful Quetzals, Curassows and a majestic Harpy Eagle. At the top of the stairs was a door that had a squared lintel made from a Mahogany log with engraved writings on it, stating the names of the present Ruler and the High Priest of the Lamanai provinces, their birth dates, and the dates when they became Ruler and High Priest. On the inside of the temple, were excessively decorated chambers, hallways and vaults for ritualistic purposes.

Deep inside the Sacred Temple was a small library with books that had been in the possession, and jealously guarded, by previous high priests of Lamanai for hundreds of years. These were very important books that had recorded the date of birth, the ascension to power, and death of previous rulers and royal families. On different shelves were books pertaining to calendrics, astrology, history, divinatory almanacs, ritualism, astronomy and prophecy. Each book had been made from the bark of the Wild Fig tree by beating it to a pulp and then strengthened with glue and white lime. Each strip of paper was folded back to back like a screen or fan to form pages then left to dry. After that, scribes laboriously wrote on it using beautiful bright colors of many shades. Inks made from minerals, vegetables, trees, and even insects were used. Some books had wooden covers while others had leather covers. They were always maintained clean and dry by their jealous guardians, the High Priests. In many Maya cities the ruler considered himself sacred and of divine descent, but not in the city of Lamanai. Throughout hundreds of years there had been a Ruler and there had been a High Priest. Presently, they were Lord Nohoch Zak Mai and Lord Sac Pec respectively. The latter also being a close personal friend of the Royal Family.

On the extreme right end of the balcony tied with a long rope was a Spider Monkey swinging and hanging from the balcony's low walls always making funny faces at, Spots the Jaguar, but always making sure to stay far away from its cage. Tuku, the juvenile Spider Monkey, was the beautiful princess of Lamanai's favorite personal pet. It had been presented to her being still a baby, only six months earlier. On the other hand Spots the beautiful Jaguar, was the direct descendant of a legendary female Jaguar, which was also called Spots that belonged to the Ruler when he was a young boy.

The young princess of the province of Dzuluinicob and city of Lamanai, Shining Blue Star, was the daughter of the ruler Nohoch Zak Mai. She was a strikingly beautiful and energetic young maiden. She loved nature and she loved taking long walks in the surrounding forest singing to the colorful birds. Spotting and naming the beautiful wild rare flowers and birds of the rainforest was a favorite pastime of hers. It was known around the sister cities that she had actually been the one that had officially named the exotic beautiful Black Orchid flower. They could never figure out why, though, since the orchid flower was purple and yellow and not black. The people really didn't care since they loved the princess very much.

The princess of Lamanai, was always followed closely, but unseen by her, by two Royal Guards whenever she ventured past the city's perimeters. She actually detested being followed or guarded. She believed that the animals she so dearly loved would protect her always. So, the guards appointed by the King himself, to follow and protect her with their life if necessary, had to do so very discreetly.

She had long silky black hair and an oval face with large light brown eyes. She was the only daughter of the ruler of Lamanai. She could always be seen around the main plaza walking her pet monkey, Tuku, and always stopping to talk to the people she encountered. She always wore a beautiful Black Orchid flower on her beautiful long rich black shiny hair. Apart from loving to study the behavior of small wild animals and identifying the flora surrounding the city, her real love and interest had always been reading and she had ample knowledge in geography, history, and astronomy among other subjects. All this had been duly observed by her parents, the high priest and his acolytes. She also loved music and she particularly loved the soothing relaxing, mystical sounds of the flute. Her mother, who also loved the flute and could master it from a very young age, would always say to her that the musical sounds of the flute accompanied by turtle shells percussions "is a wonderful experience given to the Maya people by the gods, designed to uplift their consciousness in magical ways".

Shining Blue Star believed it in her heart and she would spend hours listening to her mom play the flute while she accompanied her with percussion made from a dried calabash gourd with tiny pebbles inside. Depending on the song being played, she would sometimes use the turtle shell or the rain stick percussion. The rain stick percussion was a hollowed stick, covered on opposite sides; with corn pieces inside that when turned upside down it made a noise like rain falling. She could also play many songs on her mother's flute.

From a very tender age, princess Shining Blue Star, just loved to take long walks in the countryside with the High Priest whom she called "uncle" and question him about nature and its history. She particularly loved to question him about the various books he so jealously guarded in his library. Appreciating her interest, the wise old High Priest, Lord Sac Pek, then took it upon himself to teach the young princess how to read and write. He also taught her almost everything she wanted to know about natural history and other important subjects like astronomy and mathematics. The princess loved this so very much that every day she found time; she would go running to seek her "Uncle" to have him explain the subjects she really loved. She was a wonderful artist and she loved to sketch or draw the flora and fauna of the rainforest. So far, in her journal, she had documented two hundred and forty-two different bird species she had spotted in the forest surrounding her city. She had also recorded forty-eight mammals, which included the Jaguar and four other cat species. She had documented sixty-one reptiles including two crocodile species, many snakes and two species of Iguanas. The young princess had also counted four hundred and fifty insect species so far. Her favorite, the orchids and bromeliads, she had documented two hundred and thirty-three ones so far including the Black Orchid. All this she had drawn or sketched and documented in her personal journal.

Many times the High Priest Lord Sac Pek had mentioned to the King and Queen how extremely intelligent the princess was and that she could very well someday become the wise and beloved ruler of Lamanai or some other great city. The King and Queen of course, were delighted with this revelation from the Holy Man. The beautiful princess, Shining Blue Star, was now eleven years old and she was loved dearly by her parents, the High Priest, the Royal Guards, the people of Lamanai and of all the surrounding provinces.

Not far away, in a modest but beautiful house early that morning young Box Balam was very excited and looked forward to when he would be summoned in front of the High Priest that day. It was very early still as he lay on his hammock, identifying the different bird calls and bird songs he had learned to imitate since he was seven years old. It was as if he could hear the morning *Chacte* birds singing louder and more beautiful than ever before. It was as if they knew today was a special day for him and they had come in full force to serenade him with their sweet songs.

"Today is the day." He said silently to himself as he observed a spider weaving its nest on the ceiling of his thatch roof.

"More good luck to me." He thought, as he saw the spider walking around spinning and weaving its shiny silk. For the Maya People it was always considered lucky to have a spider weave its nest inside your room. Of course it would later be gently removed and put outside, but good luck, it was believed, would already be with the person who first saw it.

"I am so lucky already that my birthday fell on the day of the Luum Mak ceremonies". He said softly and happily to himself. "Today is also the day I will be selected to play for the royal Pok-A-Tok team." He said a little bit louder than he really wanted to. Every year a specific day was chosen for the Luum Mak ceremonies and on this year that special day was chosen, coincidentally, on Box's birthday.

Even though Box Balam almost mastered his father's craft as a sculptor and mason, his passion and dream was to one day be selected as a ball player for the Royal Team of his beloved city. Many of his friends, cousins, and other boys of his age and older, today would be appointed to their different professions and or occupations that they would be practicing for their city and people. The High Priest and his Chilams were the ones who throughout hundreds if not thousands of years were the ones to appropriately appoint them, not the ruler or the chiefs of their clans.

Architects, engineers, sculptors, healers, dentists, painters, farmers, merchants, athletes, and soldiers were some of the professions the boys could be appointed to. Some of them already mastered one of these occupations, by learning it from either his father or a close relative. One of the boys, who was a direct descendant of the High Priest, would be initiated in the study of ritualism, calendrics, astrology, writing and mathematics. He would be appointed directly to the High Priest, Lord Sac Pek, as one of his Acolytes or Chilams. Among other sacred duties he would be in charge of documenting the history of Lamanai and trained in the art of predicting natural occurrences like hurricanes and eclipses. After years of intensive spiritual training he would be able to read and write books. He would also be able to plot the cycle of the heavenly bodies, make calendars and instruct his people when was best, to plant, reap, get married, travel, or even go to war, among other sacred duties.

Most of the soldiers were also members of the Royal Ball team and they were honored and held in high regards by the Maya People of Lamanai, Hol Patin, Caracol, Altun Ha, Tikal, Xunantunich, Copan and other Maya cities far and near.

Box Balam's family house was situated adjacent a beautiful raised plaza or courtyard, The Clouds Window clan's plaza. It was here where he lived with his parents, brother, and two sisters. Box and his brother shared a bedroom while his sisters shared another, his father and mother had the biggest room of the house. The kitchen was located in a separate hut beside the main house. The kitchen like the main house was made from Palmetto poles lashed together with the very strong Ti-Tai vine that grew abundantly in the rain forest. The roof was thatched with Palmetto leaves. Both kitchen and house was beautifully plastered with White Lime mixed with *Sascab*. Sascab was a white chalky soil brought from the hills south of Lamanai which was also used for road construction.

Colorful paintings surrounded the outside wall of their home, every drawing and painting telling a story about one of their ancestors' great heroic accomplishments. Many other similar houses and huts surrounded the same plaza all belonging to the same clan. All the residents were related to Box Balams family either by blood or by marriage.

His older brother, Big Tapir's house was situated just beside theirs. He was married to a beautiful girl from Holpatin and he had recently been appointed warrior chief to the Royal Jaguar Order of Soldiers of the Royal Army. Having been appointed by the ruler himself, after proving himself a leader in making wise decisions in military tactics, he could have taken up residence in the residential area of the Royal Palace, but Big Tapir chose, rather, to live with his own Clouds Window Clan courtyard area. His walls were also beautifully painted with pictures of historic battles and ball games. Everywhere around the palaces, temples and ceremonial plazas of Lamanai were similar other courtyard or plazas surrounded by houses belonging to other clans.

The drizzle had stopped and mighty Kinich Ahau was shining brightly giving life and reviving every living thing on Mother Earth. Kinich Ahau was one of the mightiest of all Maya gods and the most revered. As evaporation began, more humidity was added to the air, but it was welcomed by the people of Lamanai; it only proved that it was going to be a perfect day for the sacred ceremony and celebration. It was about ten minutes past six when Box heard his mother calling him from the kitchen area.

"Box! Box!" His mother, Lady Tzuk called. "Wake up boy! Do you not remember what day it is today?"

"Get up and go wash yourself Box, and please wake your little brother and sisters too, you all have a lot to do today!" She said loudly as she stirred a pot of freshly cooked stew she was preparing for breakfast.

Box Balam didn't have to be told twice, he sprang up from his hammock at the same time calling to his younger brother and sisters to wake up. Box Balam adjusted his loin cloth with a string, grabbed his towel and tunic, some soap made from roots and aromatic herbs and gave the normal greeting to his mother by touching his heart with his right thumb and politely bowing and saying good morning. It was an ancient tradition that children greet all their grown up families this way. When greeting strangers and members of other clans they would place their open right palm in their heart area then recite the traditional greeting. For Royalty and the High Priest they would kneel on their right knee, bow their heads, place their right hands across their chest then recite the traditional greeting.

After getting a good morning and a happy birthday from his mother he made himself towards the bath area. It was a small artificial pond plastered with white lime to keep the water clean and fresh.

Beside the pond was a small hut made of stone, a drain behind it led waste water towards the lagoon. Inside the hut was a hearth always lit with fire so that any time of day there was hot water that could be used for bathing but Box always preferred to use the fresh sparkling water from the pond. The small artificial pond was situated about fifty feet behind the family house. It was surrounded with *Ramon*, Mahogany, *Madre Cacao* and *Pixoy* trees. A huge and gigantic *Bukut* tree with beautiful pink flowers was also growing not too far away. Aromatic shrubs and colorful flowers had been planted by Box's mother around the pond. The ponds water was sparkling clean and it had captured more rainwater from last night's rain.

As Box washed himself he couldn't help thinking about the day, years ago, when while playing ball with his cousins and friends, his beloved uncle Crocodile Tooth said to him, "Box Balam I notice you have a gift for playing Pok-A-Tok if you keep on playing that way someday you might very well be selected to play with the Royal Team."

That was the incentive that Box needed, from that day on he practiced harder and dreamed that one day, like his favorite uncle, he could play Pok-A-Tok in the Royal Ball Court of his beloved city. His uncle, Crocodile Tooth, had been a brave soldier, talented athlete, and great ball player. His father in the other hand had pursued a more artistic career and became a talented sculptor and mason. After many victorious battles against the foreign armies of the Far North cities, from beyond Chac'temal, Crocodile Tooth had been appointed warrior chief of the Royal Army of Lamanai. He was widely known and respected throughout many Maya cities because of his prowess and courage in defending the cities from foreign armies and hostile invaders from the Far North cities.

The city of Altun Ha, which was about a day's journey by foot from Lamanai, had erected a special monument honoring Crocodile Tooth the great retired warrior and Pok A Tok player. Many years ago, he had helped repeal an invasion from the army of the Far North. The Ruler of Lamanai, Lord Nohoch Zak Mai, was always happy to help Lamanai's sister city, Altun Ha, in whatever way necessary. One day he was asked for help by the ruler of Altun Ha, Lord Choc Chen, to repeal a small army of marauders coming by way of the great waters, the sea. The ruler of Lamanai then decided to send his best army of warriors led by chief Crocodile Tooth to help the people of Altun Ha drive back the invaders. Crocodile Tooth's specialized war company was widely known as "The Jaguar Order of Soldiers" named after the clan of the beloved ruler Lord Nohoch Zak Mai. They had returned home victorious and heroes.

Chief Crocodile Tooth was honorably retired now, but Box and his cousins just loved hearing his tales of war and adventure. He would usually show them a scar in his body and begin by saying, "many years ago while,"—and he then would entertain them with one of his stories of adventure. He had, though, a big ugly scar on his left shoulder, an old battle wound that had almost cost him his life. This was the wound that had forced him to end his military career causing him to semi-retire from the army. He rarely spoke about that scar or the battle that had caused it. All he told and what the people knew was that he had been badly hurt on his shoulder during a battle against invaders from the Far North while helping defend their allied city of Chac'temal. For reasons known only to him he chose never to talk about that particular battle. Whenever his nephews and nieces would point to the scar on his shoulder he would always say, "some other day I'll tell you," then he would immediately begin a story about ancient warriors and ball players. They particularly loved hearing stories from the Sacred Book of their people—The Popol Vuh. Specially the part about the Hero Twins, Hunapuh and Xbalanque, winning a game of Pok A Tok, the sacred ball game of their people, against the Lords of the Underworld.

Even though the sun was shining brightly, under the canopy of the rainforest was a bit dark and mysterious looking. The high canopy of the Rain Forest shielded the sun from the lower parts of the rainforest. Nonetheless, it was still very hot and humid. The Black Howler monkeys were howling louder than usual, alpha males warning each other to stay away from their territories.

It was one of these days that Box and his father Sky Balam had been out hunting for the coveted game bird the Curassow. Whilst returning back home, with two fat

Curassows hanging over his shoulders, Box decided to ask his father about the story behind Crocodile Tooth's big scar on his left shoulder. At first Sky Balam was a bit reluctant in telling Box about it. It was a story told only between adults but after much insistence on Box's part, and because Box would soon become a man on the fast approaching day of the Luum Mak, he decided to tell him.

Sky Balam explained that his brother, Chief Crocodile Tooth, three of his most courageous officers, and some of his men were ambushed by enemy soldiers twice their numbers while they were camping on a heavily wooded area around Chac'temal. After fiercely trying to defend themselves, Chief Crocodile Tooth and all of his men had been subdued and left for dead. The enemy attackers had then fled into the darkness. A brother and a cousin of Crocodile Tooth had been killed in this battle and their demise lay heavily on the shoulders of the aging chief. Even though he and his soldiers were awarded with the highest honor and his heroic battle was immortalized in a Stella, carved on a monolith by the most talented sculptors, he always blamed himself in the loss of his brother, cousin and some of his most seasoned warriors. He believed, that he had been too trusting with soldiers of the allied armies not knowing there was a spy in their midst, and as the chief, he put all the blame on himself on the surprise attack. He always thought he should have known better. He believed he should have been more cautious and less trusting with soldiers who weren't on his army.

As the story goes, Chac'temal was betrayed to the enemies by Red Cloud, the wicked brother of Lord Great Mot Mot, the ruler of Chac'temal and its provinces. Red Cloud was next in line to be ruler of Chac'temal if Great Mot Mot should die and it was common knowledge everywhere, that he wanted his ruling brother dead so he could inherit the throne of Chac'temal and later join forces and be in alliance with the Northern Empires. Crocodile Tooth's army had foiled Red Cloud's attempt to kill Lord Great Mot Mot his loyal royal guards and later claim the throne of Chac'temal.

It was still early in the afternoon but it was already getting dark in the rainforest when Box asked his father if he could stop to gather some ripe wild papayas. After eating a couple of the papayas, Sky Balam continued telling his son Box about Crocodile Tooth.

He had told him that it was later discovered that Red Cloud, had secretly instructed his personal guards to attack and kill Crocodile Tooth and his men at three in the morning when they were resting after the battle that drove back the Northern Army that wanted to invade Chac'temal and had caused the demise of many great warriors of Chief Crocodile Tooth's army. It was then decided that Red Cloud's family and guards loyal to him should be banished forever from Chac'temal and all its allied territories and cities forever. An urgent meeting had been held in the city of Holpatin by all the High Priests and ambassadors of all the allied cities including Xunantunich, Cahal-Pech, Caracol, Altun Ha, Lamanai, Tikal and Copan. It was then determined that because of his evil actions Red Cloud, his family and two of his guards loyal to him should be exiled forever from Chac'temal and its allied territories. Only because he came from a Royal Lineage and two of the ambassadors and his brother had spoken on his behalf, was spared from being sacrificed to the Gods.

They were escorted by the Royal Soldiers out of the city making sure they only had enough food for three days. They were not allowed to take any of their royal treasures or clothing. All of their possessions were placed in the center of the main plaza, and with all the people watching including Red Cloud himself, was completely burned. Not even his clothes, kitchen bowls, plate, and other utensils survived. They were either all destroyed burned or distributed amongst the people. The very same day he was expelled, the ruler ordered Red Cloud's family residential area in the Royal Palace be demolished and a new addition be built for his eldest son. Red Cloud had indeed paid a high price for his treason. It was rumored that he, his family and his group of loyal guards had sought refuge in a city in the Northern Territories. A traveling merchant had confirmed seeing them there and he also said that Red Cloud always talked about getting his revenge with his older brother for sending him on exile and Crocodile Tooth for foiling his attempt in becoming the ruler of Chac'temal. The merchant also reported that he and his son, along with other mercenaries he had recruited, with the promise of riches after he dethroned his brother from Chac'temal, was training with the Armies of the Far North.

As Box and his father continued walking towards their city and their clan's plaza, feeling very tired after a day of hunting successfully, Sky Balam continued telling Box the story about the city of Chac'temal, Its past ruler and the present ruler Great Macaw.

Many years had gone by and the rulers of the Allied Cities had all forgotten about Red Cloud and his threat to one day come back for revenge against his brother and Crocodile Tooth. For many years now there had not been any attacks by foreign armies against any of the allied cities. The rulers and high priests now believed that the attacks throughout those years were instigated by the wicked Red Cloud. The allied territories had been enjoying peace for many years now. Great Mot Mot, once ruler of Chac'temal, was dead for four years now. His son Great Macaw had ascended to the throne of Chac'temal and like his father was a just and kind ruler, the people loved him very much. Under the new ruler, the city and its villages had continued to prosper. The farmers and the High Priest, who instructed them when was the best time to plant and harvest, worked very hard so that their *Chultuns*, their underground bottle shaped pits used as cisterns and storage, were always filled with grains and food so the people were always well fed and happy. The city's merchants always traded honestly with other traveling merchants and they always held a good peaceful relations with their entire sister cities.

Like everywhere else though, there were always thieves and robbers, but Great Macaw's Royal Guards always made sure the citizens were well protected. Great Macaw also knew the story about his uncle's betrayal to his people. It was recorded in the sacred books by the Royal Scribes. He also knew about his uncles threats. So he always kept his Royal Guards and army in a state of war readiness.

He never forgot his father's last words as he lay on his death bed with Copal incensories burning on each corner of the room. "My son, my beloved son," He had whispered in his ears. "As I go to join our ancestors, don't ever forget that your uncle is very wicked, he will surely come back someday when he learns that I am dead, to try to dethrone you. Please, be always prepared and never trust him." As the Royal Healer wiped the old ruler's forehead with a damp cloth, Great Macaw held his hands tightly and with tears in his eyes he said, "I won't father, I promise, and I will always be prepared." Lord Great Mot Mot looked at young Great Macaw and added, "don't be sad my son I am now going to where my ancestors are, I will be happy there, but," He had continued, "as I travel through the nine chambers of Xibalba to be reunited with my ancestors in eternal peace in heaven, along with Hunab Ku almighty, we will be looking over you, our family and our beloved city Chac'temal. Be strong and firm but rule our people justly, wisely and with love so the gods can smile upon you and your people." Those were the last words of the beloved and wise ruler of the city of Chac'temal and its provinces.

The great ruler was interred deep inside a temple that had been constructed specially for him years before he died. Beside him, in his sarcophagus, were several polychrome vases filled with chocolate drink and several pottery bowls containing food and water. His personal shield and weapons were also laid beside him. He was laid to rest in his full Royal Regalia, around his neck was a collar of two hundred jade beads and most of his fingers had jade rings and two flower shaped ear flares adorned his ears. His body was wrapped in Jaguar skins and as per tradition on burial rituals, a single big round shiny green jade bead had been placed inside his mouth to ensure that he could purchase food in the afterlife. His body had been sprinkled with cinnabar as per Maya custom and clay and jade effigies had been set all over the burial chamber. Outside of the burial chamber three young warriors had been sacrificed. They had weapons in their hands and they were intended to guard and serve the great dead ruler of Chac'temal, Lord Great Mot Mot, in the afterlife. The temple was then sealed with stones and mortar and the Royal Sculptors began carving the image of the great ruler and his life history in huge monoliths to be placed in front of the temple where he was buried.

Sky Balam concluded his story by saying, "I hope that the malicious Red Cloud is now dead or at least that he forgets about Chac'temal. We really don't need another war right now, son. There were too many useless losses of lives on both armies. Every boy your age must have a family killed in that war. I believe that is the reason my brother prefers not to tell young children about that particular battle since he was also almost killed there because of treachery too." Box agreed by nodding his head. He then thanked his father with all his heart for telling him the true story behind the huge scar on Crocodile Tooth's shoulder.

Box then shifted the two heavy birds from one shoulder to the next while his father carried the bow and the quiver of arrows. He now walked with pride and feeling very important, now that he also knew about Crocodile Tooth's scar and the Battle of Chac'temal. He felt like a real man now. What a story to share with his good friend Red Cat.

About ten minutes before arriving home Box sighted an armadillo in the distance. Knowing how much his mother loved armadillo meat he decided to take a shot at it. He walked carefully and silently with his father's bow and arrow towards the armadillo feeding under a tree. As soon as he prepared to sling his bow and shoot the armadillo, a great and huge Harpy Eagle swooped down and grasped the armadillo with its powerful claws taking it away. Sky Balam laughed softly as he saw the look of surprise and astonishment in his son's face.

"It's o. k, its o.k. son," Sky Balam said amidst laughter. "The bird beat you to it. You were a bit slow with the bow and arrow, but let me tell you another true story," he said after he stopped laughing. "This weapon, the bow and arrow, unlike the spears, axes and clubs is not an original weapon used by our ancestors. It was adopted many years ago by our ancestors after it was found on dead enemies of our people on a battle many, many, years ago. It has proved to be a very good weapon for long distance battle or even hunting, but it is not in our blood, Box. I was observing you tactically approaching the armadillo and even though you could have shot it without approaching it, you decided to go even closer to it. You know my son," he continued. "It will always be on our blood to do close quarter battle against our enemies or strike a prey from close. Using a club and or spear will always be in our blood. The reason, I believe, you tried to get as close as you could, but the eagle beat you to it." He laughed some more.

It was almost dark when Box and his father arrived at their house with the two birds they had killed. As Box walked towards the wash area, deep in thought, his mother immediately began preparing the birds for their supper. Box had always been extremely proud of his uncle Chief Crocodile Tooth but after hearing the story about the Battle of Chac'temal and his uncle's heroic accomplishment there, he was even more so. Deep in his heart he longed to one day become a hero like his uncle.

Three weeks later he was by his family bathing pond getting ready for the ceremony that would declare him a full grown man.

CHAPTER TWO ..

After taking a bath, Box Balam fell on one knee, put his right arm across his chest and silently gave thanks to Hunab Ku almighty, the Supreme God, for this wonderful and glorious day. He also thanked Chac, the Rain God for stopping its blessed waters from falling from the sky for today. He specially thanked Kinich Ahau for shining so brightly giving the people of Lamanai a perfect opportunity to celebrate the *Luum Mak* ceremony the way it was intended.

As he rose from his kneeling position, his highly trained eyes caught a glimpse of movement behind the trees in the forest beyond. It was as if an animal or maybe someone had moved in the bushes around the trees beyond. The feeling and sensation of something or someone watching him was very strong, but when he stopped to further observe the area he had seen the movement, he could see nothing else. He dismissed it from his mind as a wild and elusive animal looking for a meal. Very rarely had a Jaguar or Puma or other wild animal ever attacked a human in that area but it was always wise to be cautious. The Maya elders always said that a wild animal is more afraid of people than we are of them, but it was smart to always be careful. An injured animal, or if you venture too close to where they keep their young ones, will attack you. It was very rare, but old Jaguars who could not hunt anymore would sometimes attack a small person or child who had ventured too far away into the jungle by himself.

Box Balam was a tall athletic boy, at fourteen years of age he was five feet six inches in height. He was already as tall as or taller than most men of his clan. As he walked back towards his house he saw his father, Sky Balam, walking towards him. Today, for the ceremony, he was dressed in his full ceremonial regalia as was appropriate for a well known talented artisan of his status. As they approached each other Box Balam politely bowed to his father at the same time placing his right thumb on his heart and saying, "greetings my father, good morning to you and may you walk in peace always," reciting the traditional greetings a young person gives to his parents and elders. His father greeted him in return and placed both of his arms on Box's shoulders.

"Box," he said. "I wanted to speak alone to you before you go in front of our Halach Uinich, our High Priest and his Chilams," he continued. "Remember, it doesn't matter which profession is chosen for you, and you must accept it with honor, yes, you have the right to protest and refuse your first offer and ask for another appointment but I tell you now, don't. It is always of great respect to the ruler when a man accepts his first appointment given to him after the Luum Mak."

Sky Balam looked deep into his sons eyes and very gently said, "I know I thought you well in the skills of masonry and sculpture and you were always my best student, I also know that you are a good hunter and skilled ball player,

I know too that you dream of becoming a ball player but please heed my advice, don't get disappointed if you are not chosen for the Royal Team, you are young and will have other opportunities."

"Yes father," answered Box, "I won't disappoint you."

Box Balam knew that what his father really wanted was for him to follow in his footsteps. Even as a young child his father had always told him how proud he would be if he also became an artisan. Box admired his father's famous sculptures and paintings very much and he was very much proud of him but he had other dreams and he really wanted to be a soldier and ball player and he knew his father would support him on this. Countless times he had seen his father discussing his career with his uncle Crocodile Tooth. He also knew that his father would never try to influence his distant cousin on his behalf, who was one of the holy men in charge of appointing the young boys to their sacred professions.

After he was dismissed by his father he ate a hearty breakfast prepared by his mother and sister Ek Balam. It consisted of smoked Armadillo stewed with Cohune nuts oil. Fried beans, Chili and herbs in baked mashed tomatoes eaten with corn tortillas. Fresh fruit juice and some boiled sweet potato and manioc soaked in honey was also laid on the table.

Squash, Manioc, Sweet Potato, Beans, Tomato, Papayas, and Chili were only a few of the agricultural products enjoyed by the Maya people. The one most enjoyed by the peasants and elites alike though, was Maize, "Sun beams of The Gods" they called it. The Maya people could prepare innumerable wonderful and exquisite dishes with Maize or Corn. Today, for the first time though, Box will be tasting *Cho'co'latle* (Chocolate) a drink made from the Cacao Beans sweetened with honey. A drink reserved for royalty, high priests, the elite and the gods. In very rare occasions, it was also enjoyed by the peasants and the common people. Every year though it was served to the young men in their initiation into adulthood during the sacred *Luum Mak* ceremonies.

For young Box and his colleagues drinking chocolate was like drinking money for the cacao beans were also used by his people for purchasing goods. Box remembered one day his mother paying with cacao beans to a hunter for a deer he had just killed and cleaned. It was as if for the Maya people 'money grew on trees.' No big wonder the Cacao crops were controlled by the Royal Families and not the farmers themselves. So, it was only the Royalty and the very rich that could enjoy a full gourd of chocolate drink. Another first for Box and his colleagues would be to taste *Balche wine,* a very small quantity, of course. *Balche* is a potent intoxicating drink made from the bark of the *Balche* tree soaked in honey and water to ferment.

While Box Balam and all boys of his age were preparing for the ceremonies that morning, from very early, princess Shining Blue Star, Princess of Lamanai, with Tuku her very excited and playful pet monkey in tow, walked around the plazas where the celebrations were to be held. She spoke to the women preparing food as they proudly handed her some of whatever they were cooking for her and her monkey to taste. As she walked around the plazas she was politely greeted by everyone including the men building thatch shades around the plazas. She spent a long time talking to the musicians that had travelled to Lamanai from distant lands for this very special occasion. She questioned them about some of the musical instruments they had brought and that were strange to her. Some of the young musicians inspired by her radiant beauty even serenaded her with a couple songs of love. Some of these love songs she knew the lyrics very well, since her mother had been singing it to her since she was a baby.

Most of the Maya people were polyglots; they spoke different dialects, including the princess. So in every opportunity she had, she would converse with other Maya people, in their dialect, that came from different lands and spoke a different dialect than hers. In this occasion she had the opportunity to practice different dialects since many different people had come from far away in the high lands of the west and other far away Maya Cities, to celebrate with the people of Lamanai. Performers, dignitaries, merchants and musicians included. They all proudly wore their traditional dresses, and the singers proudly sang in their own dialects. The young princess was delighted in hearing about their interesting beautiful cities, peoples, customs and listening to their love songs and stories. Her mother had once told her that, hundreds of years ago, the Maya People spoke only one Mayan language. But, because of war within cities and provinces and because some cities were built far away from one another, one common language developed and evolved into various dialects throughout hundreds of years.

Early one morning as the princess was taking her daily walk besides a fallowed field singing a love song that was composed by a Lamanai artist a hundred years ago which's name no one remembered. She was admiring the beautiful colorful morning song birds when she was joined by the High Priest Lord Sac Pek. Even the ever keen eyesight of Lord Sac Pek could not detect the two well camouflaged Royal Guards that always followed the princess around. He was amazed on their tactical prowess; and that brought him a great sense of relief knowing that the future ruler of

Lamanai was well protected. He knew that these guards of the Jaguar Order were well trained and they were considered to be some of the best tactical warriors for hundreds of miles around within the Sister Cities armies. As he approached the princess, he whistled, imitating a White Crowned Parrot, the young princess immediately recognized the special call and she responded with a low guttural call imitating the colorful Keel Billed Toucan. Even though she had not seen him, she knew it was her "uncle" Sac. Her calling back was the invitation for him to join her. The high priest was one of the few people she loved to take long walks with. She immensely enjoyed it since she learned so much from him.

Recognizing medicinal plants as well as toxic ones were only a few of the things she had learned from him. The dreaded straight growing Black Poison Wood tree was one of the first toxic plants she learned to recognize. He always insisted that apart from learning the names of beautiful flowers, birds, trees and animals she learned to distinguish between "bad and good" animals and insects, especially snakes. He had once pointed out a King snake to her and had said, "See how beautiful that snake is, Shining Blue Star? Well, they are the same colors as the very venomous Coral snake. Always be aware that both snakes are equally important to the environment even though, one can kill you with a single strike while the other will only pretend to be the venomous one. Take note where the ring colors on its body meet," he said, "and you will be certain you won't be endangering yourself by handling the wrong one."

"Remember," he continued saying, "there are many, many more non-venomous snakes than venomous snakes living in our rain forests; but always be cautious when taking your walks. Be especially cautious of the most venomous and dangerous of them all the Fer-De-Lance snake. The one with its head resembling a spear head and with a yellow jaw," he advised the young adventure spirited young princess.

After taking a long walk and being silent for fifteen minutes just enjoying the calls of the wild they sat down under the shade of a towering huge Mahogany tree. A tree that was probably there even before the first permanent building was constructed in Lamanai hundreds of years ago. It was a majestic tree and a huge Harpy Eagle had built its nest on its highest branch. The height of the tree re-assured the majestic bird that its young ones would be safe from predators.

After resting for a while, a beautiful bright white and yellow butterfly flew past the High Priest and the princess. "See that butterfly," the High Priest said to the princess, "it's one of the most fragile of God's creatures it will only live for a few days, yet, before it dies, it will make sure its generation continues to survive. We, the Maya People, have always been the same. For generations our ancestors have passed on their knowledge to us, re-assuring our survival. Yes, there have been wars and while I personally hate it I believe that sometimes it is necessary for the continued survival of our people and their knowledge." The old wise Holy Man looked at the young bright princess and continued saying, "I know you are young and at this time you may not fully understand what I am about to tell you, but you are very smart and will one day understand. What I say to you should not be repeated to anyone." The young Princess only nodded in agreement and she became even more attentive. "The future has very bad things in store for our people." The old high priest said. "Not in my lifetime nor yours, but, not too far away in our future, our civilization will be destroyed. At this time I don't know the real causes but I have seen it in the stars. The stars tell me princess," he said as he looked towards the lagoon where a group of children were swimming, laughing and splashing water to one another, "that in the very near future our great civilization will collapse. Our great cities will be abandoned and the jungle will once more claim its lands. I have also seen it many times in visions when conducting personal rituals to our gods. I have consulted with other high priests, but no other one has had this visions and no one believes our mighty empire can ever collapse."

The young princess held the old man's hand and gently said, "I do believe you uncle Sac and I am sure, so does my father and mother. My father has repeatedly mentioned that your predictions and prophecies have always come to pass." The princess had an expression of concern and surprise in her face even as she said this. In her young innocent age it was hard for her to believe that the wonderful and beautiful cities she had visited, including the one she was born, may one day be only ruins shrouded by jungle. But young as she was she believed it because the Holy Man and High Priest of Lamanai had always been right.

From where they sat, under the majestic old Mahogany Tree which soared over a hundred and ten feet high with its branches above the canopy of the rainforest, the eastern top side of the Sacred Temple could be seen. Visible, so that travelers coming to Lamanai could see it from afar, was a huge Long Count Calendar. It was carved beside the Emblem Glyph of the city which was a crocodile with the God of wisdom and writing, the Supreme God, in its open mouth on the eastern top wall of the sacred temple.

"See that Long Count Calendar, Shining Blue Star," said the old Holy Man as he pointed towards the visible part of the Sacred Temple. It will end on a windy day on the last days of the month of December of the year two thousand twelve. It also coincides with the day when our God Kinich Ahau and our planet will be aligned with the center of the Milky Way Galaxy. Who knows what changes there will be in our Earth? Will there be natural disasters greater than ones humanity has ever seen? Will humanity be destroyed so there could be a new beginning on earth and the beginning of a new Long Count Calendar? Only our supreme god mighty Hunab Ku can answer these questions. There is only one thing I can tell you, though, princess," he said sadly as if the end of the Long Count Calendar would be tomorrow, "Our previous High Priests throughout our history knew it and I know it and it is recorded in our Holy Books."

Lord Sac Pec, other High Maya Priests and the Maya People actually used three different calendars. The Long Count, the Haab, and the Tzolkin. The Long Count was used for historical purposes since they could define any date for millennia in the past as well as in the future. The Haab was more a civil calendar and it was a three hundred sixty days calendar consisting of eighteen periods of twenty days. Five days were normally added at the end of the Haab year so it can be synchronized with the solar year. The Tzolkin Calendar in the other hand was used specifically for ceremonial purposes. It consisted of twenty periods of thirteen days. The Tzolkin Calendar went through a complete cycle of two hundred sixty days and was associated with the orbit of the planet Venus. All three calendars were equally important to the Maya High Priests and the Maya People. Apart from everything else Lord Sac Pec was actually one of the most knowledgeable and respected astronomer of all of the Maya provinces. In his library he actually kept several calendars that had been drawn on paper hundreds of years ago by previous High Priests whose names were also recorded on them.

"Who knows," he continued saying, as his eyes followed the beautiful butterfly. "Our demise may come about because we are destroying the rainforest." The butterfly perched on the leaf of a small shrub, stretched and flapped its bright yellow wings showing off to the world then flew deep into the forest.

"The rain forest has given us life for thousands of years, yet, we continue to destroy it. From it we get our food, medicines and shelters. Yes, good things come from the rainforest but many bad things like diseases come from it too. The demise of our civilization may come about, princess, because the earth might take revenge on humanity for destroying its eco-systems. Who knows what diseases we are awakening when we totally destroy a piece of the rainforest? It could be that a disease may emerge from the rainforest that may have no cure. Mother Earth will be taking her vengeance on us by killing many of us with its deadly diseases. There is very little the gods can do against the wrath of Mother Earth. But, be at ease princess Blue Shining Star for this will not happen for several hundreds of years as predicted on the Holy Book."

As the sun got higher and the air started to get more humid the High Priest stood up and motioned the princess to do the same. The princess had been silent for a long time, deep in thoughts, and her beautiful face had a worried expression. "I understand your concern and worries princess," he said. When I first got this revelation from my grandfather and later from the gods, I too became worried for a long time; but you will get over it. Remember, this information belongs only to very special people and I have seen in the stars that you will one day become a powerful ruler. The reason I share this information with you." As the princess rose from the ground clearing dry grass that had stuck to her long brightly colored embroidered skirt, she looked up at the beautiful blue sky and said," Uncle Sac, today is much too beautiful a day for me to worry about the distant future. Please, accompany me to the palace for breakfast I am sure my parents will be happy to see you. She laughed loudly, momentarily forgetting the darkness the future had in store for her beloved people, as she saw a baby Black Howler Monkey swinging in the branches above, miss a branch, but expertly hanging on to another one below, with his mothers clearly roaring at him for not being careful as she had taught him.

The old wise Holy Man looked at the princess, Shining Blue Star, as she laughed at the baby monkey who was trying very hard to control its awkward balance on the tree top. He smiled as he reminisced, "the innocence of the young, how wonderful. It seems like yesterday I was behaving the same way". Holding hands, they then both walked towards the Royal Palace, while Blue Shining Star hummed the tune of an ancient love song. Far away she could see a group of boys playing Pok-A-Tok, including young Box whom she really didn't know but had seen practicing many times before. She actually just loved to watch the young boys play ball.

Before midday, twenty-four young boys, including Box Balam, were already kneeling in the middle of the Sacred Plaza in front of the Sacred Temple. It was a beautiful day and the sun was shining brightly. All the buildings around the plaza had been freshly painted with beautiful bright colors. The plaza itself, where they were kneeling, had recently been coated with white lime, and it gleamed with the rays of the sun. All around, the plaza was decorated with aromatic wild and domesticated flowers. The unmistakable sweet aroma of the smoke of the sacred *Copal* Incense hung in the air. The twenty four boys waited nervously with anticipation, on one knee. Their heads were bowed, and their right hands rested across their chest until the Ruler and the High Priest, sitting in the balcony of the Sacred Temple, would ask them to rise.

Most of them had their shiny black hair up to their shoulders. Some of them had it loose while others had it in braids. Every one of them, though, had a shiny white bead braided onto their hair and it dangled on the right side of their head. Some of the boys were crossed-eyed. They were not born this way; when still an infant a small bead had been attached from their hair, dangling in front of their eyes so that they could become crossed-eyed. This was some of the Maya People's ideas in making their children more beautiful. Not all, but many people actually desired that their child be born crossed-eyed. They considered it a thing of beauty. All of the boys had a piece of white cloth on their heads. Their mothers had placed it on their heads before the Sacred Ceremonies began.

Sitting on the far end of the lower balcony were the ambassadors and delegates from other cities. Everyone was eagerly waiting for the signal from Lord Nohoch Zak May for the ceremony to commence. Lord Nohoch Zak Mai and the Queen were sitting at the centre of the upper balcony. Sitting beside the Queen was the princess. She was busy feeding her pet spider monkey, Tuku, pieces of fruit. Lord Nohoch Zak Mai was dressed in his full royal regalia. A headdress of beautiful, bright and elaborately colored plumage adorned his head and he had on a long tunic made from Jaguar skin and a cape made from Ocelot skin. In his hand he held a carved wooden scepter embedded with jewelry. The head of a Jaguar made of green Jade was attached to the top end of the scepter.

He had on huge jade ear flares inlaid with Mother of Pearl and three necklaces of glittering green jade adorned his neck, bracelets of jade and beautiful shell beads were on his wrist. His mouth sparkled with tiny jade pieces that were inlaid in his teeth and a standing Jaguar was tattooed on his chest.

The Queen and Princess were dressed in long white cotton dresses with huge colorful embroidered birds and flowers in the front and back. Above the hems and sleeves of their dresses, bright red roses had been embroidered. They both wore an orchid flower on their long black shiny hair. They both also wore jewelry of Jade and shells around their necks, wrists and ankles. They also wore long shiny green jade earrings.

Behind them, in full military ceremonial dress stood Chief Crocodile Tooth the retired military chief of the army of Lamanai and chief of the Jaguar Order Warriors, the ruler's personal Royal Guards. The High Priest, Lord Sac Pek, with his two acolytes, also called Chilams, standing behind them, was also dressed in full ceremonial dress. Far down below sitting on long benches on the left hand side of the plaza were the proud family members of the boys, kneeling in the middle of the plaza. Seated behind them were the prominent citizens of Lamanai.

On the right hand side of the sacred plaza standing at attention in their full battle order was a platoon of Royal Soldiers. Immediately in front of them was Box's brother, the present Chief of the Royal Army dressed in full military ceremonial dress. Everywhere else around the plaza were hundreds of citizens waiting for the ceremony and after that, the celebrations to begin.

At exactly midday everyone could hear the great Sacred Conch Shell blowing once more on the very top of the temple, it was blown three times, the signal for the ceremony to begin. As the Great Ruler rose from his throne everybody else rose with him, excepting the boys kneeling with their heads bowed slightly. His powerful voice could be heard everywhere around the plaza as he lifted both his hands signaling his people to be seated.

"I am sure," he said aloud, addressing the twenty four young men kneeling in the middle of the plaza, "that you boys becoming men today will make Lamanai proud. This year," he continued, "it will be a little different; today you will all be assigned a special task. You will all go on a mission that should be completed in exactly five days beginning tomorrow." He raised his scepter higher with his right hand as he continued saying, "at the end of this mission you will all be integrated into military school for military training for four weeks. At the end of these four weeks, those of you who satisfactorily finish this military course will come before me and the High Priest. Then, and only then will you be assigned to your different professions. So, new men of Lamanai, make us proud," he said in conclusion.

As the ruler sat down once again, the old High Priest, Sac Pek, and his helpers started descending the steep stairs of the Sacred Temple very slowly towards the boys. Hearing the rulers speech, only added more anxiety to the boys, even the people witnessing this special event were in awe. This was unheard of. Why should the boys go on a mission first? Why send all the boys to military school when certainly some of them would be chosen to be engineers, masons and even dentists? Nohoch Zak Mai was a wise ruler and the people of lamanai trusted his good judgment. They trusted him on why he was changing the very ancient tradition of

Luum Mak to not appoint the boys on their professions before sending them on certain missions. As the old High Priest and his Chilams approached the boys, a refreshing breeze could be felt coming from the Dzuluinicob lagoon east of the city.

As the High Priest walked in front of the two rows of slightly sweating boys kneeling silently with heads bowed, he thoroughly inspected each and every one of them. After being satisfied with their appearance and that each one still had the white bead attached to his hair, he clapped his hands three times signaling the boys to stand. Immediately the two *Chilams*, one on each row of twelve started chanting and praying, at the same time swinging a smoking Copal incensory above the boys head. One of them also held a finely carved stick with the end tail of rattle snakes attached to it. He waved it above and around their heads while sprinkling Holy Water on them. The Holy Water had been collected from the stalactites dripping water from inside caves. This Holy Water was the same water that throughout thousands of years had formed some of these magnificent stalactites and stalagmites inside the caves drip by drip by drip.

When Box turned his head slightly he could see his family beaming at him proudly. He could also see his brother, Big Tapir, in full ceremonial military regalia standing at attention, and perfectly still in front of three lines of soldiers comprising the Royal Guard of Honor also standing perfectly still. He was so proud of his brother and very much wanted to be like him. He could also see the branches of the Ramon, Mahogany and a huge Rain Tree swaying in the wind. These trees, he was told, were planted by his ancestors, The Clouds Window Clan, hundreds of years ago to give shade to the Royal Palace and Sacred

Temple. Towering over all the other trees was a huge and sacred Ceiba Tree. The Ceiba Tree represented the thirteen heavens of the Maya People. Every heaven was for a specific god. At the very top was Hunab Ku, the unseen Supreme Being, God of wisdom and writing followed by Ixchell the goddess of childbirth, medicine and weaving. All the other gods, it was believed, were offspring's of Hunab Ku and Ixchell.

After the *Chilams* finished their chant, the High Priest, tapped each boys shoulder with his left hand. He then removed the white bead that had been braided in the boy's hair since they were five years old. This was done by cutting off the piece of braided hair with a very sharp obsidian knife. Most the boys had their hair all the way to their shoulders while some of them had it even longer. The lock of hair with the white bead was then wrapped in the small piece of white cloth that had been on the boys' head; then ceremoniously presented to their mothers. This proved to her that her son was now a full grown man. This always brought tears to the proud mothers' eyes.

Then one by one the High Priest hung a necklace made from beautiful pink shell and shiny green Jade beads around each of the boy's neck. He then presented each one with a tunic made from Jaguar skin and a bow with thirteen arrows, the sign that they should only bear allegiance to the Royal Family's Jaguar Clan, his own clan, and the people and city of Lamanai. After performing all this, the High Priest and his two aides walked in front of the lines of men and facing them, the High Priest said softly, so only they could hear him, "today you become men and new citizens of our beloved city Lamanai; As you have heard, our great ruler Lord Nohoch Zak Mai, today, has decided that your appointments would come about a little differently than it has traditionally been done. You are probably wondering why we haven't presented you with your headdress feather as per tradition as you expected. Not to worry though," he continued, "after your mission you will all be presented with your feather to be worn proudly on your heads wherever you go. Tomorrow," the High Priest announced more loudly turning around so that everyone could hear him. "These new men will once more report at this same spot. They will then be divided in groups of two's and a Royal Guard will be appointed as their mentor. They will then embark on a mission that will be instructed to them by their mentors before they leave."

He once more lifted both hands as he continued, "these are the wishes of our ruler." He looked at the boys once more and gently but firmly said, "We all expect you to excel in your mission and training, good luck and the gods be with you all." All the young men crossed their hands on their chest and bowed slightly, giving the High Priest the message that they understood and accepted his orders.

Immediately after that, at the sounds of ceremonial drums beating, twenty-four young maidens not older than fourteen years of age dressed in white cotton dresses embroidered with bright red flowers came out of the Palace. Their beautiful black hair cascaded down to their waist and it glistened in the sun. They all had a yellow rose attached to the right of their heads just above their ears. Each one of them had in their hands a beautifully decorated calabash gourd filled with the drink *Cho'co'latle* sweetened with honey and whipped so that its froth rose to the rim of the gourd. Ceremoniously, every girl presented one of the boys with the deliciously wonderful drink. The beautiful young maidens stood in front of each boy smiling as they waited for them to finish drinking the chocolate drink. After that with drums beating and flutes playing the young girls, in two straight lines one behind the other disappeared into the Palace with the empty gourds in their hands.

"This is the most delicious drink I have ever had," thought Box, "with more reason I want to be in the Royal Ball Team." Rumors had it, that among other prizes, every time a team won, they were all presented with a bowl of frothing Chocolate Drink.

He was still licking his lips when once more the girls appeared, this time wearing a long sky-blue dress decorated with colorful birds, Jaguars and monkeys embroidered around the hems and the sleeves. A long white shawl also hung over their shoulders and a Red Rose decorated the right side of their long black hair. This time their shiny black hair was twisted in one single braid that fell all the way down to their waist. Every one of them, once more, held a different bowl in their hands and this time approaching a different young man. As one of the girls approached him, Box Balam couldn't help noticing how beautiful she was. Her long silky black hair, he noticed, was braided a little different than the other girls for it was also decorated with an iridescent feather of the majestic Quetzal Bird. Her sparkling big brown eyes looked straight into his. Her lips were painted red and she had the most beautiful smile Box had ever seen. The lovely girl continued smiling as she handed Box the gourd which this time, was filled with *Balche*. He smiled in return bowing slightly in gratitude.

"What is your name?" He whispered to her as he put the gourd to his lip. As he tasted the burning potent *Balche*, wine he knew that this was one drink he didn't care for; but to prove he was a man he drank it all without frowning.

"Ixchel Quetzal", she whispered softly back to him as he handed her back the empty gourd. As all the girls turned

41

together and headed back to the Royal Palace. Box's sight not once left her, until she disappeared into the Palace. "Wonderful," thought Box, "she has the name of the greatest and most powerful goddess, Ixchell, I love her already." All of this did not go unnoticed by Box's sister Ek Balam who was one of the girls serving the men and who also attended school with Ixchel Quetzal.

"Take your time, new citizens of Lamanai," said the High Priest addressing Box Balam and his colleagues, "this drink is *Balche,* a potent intoxicating drink, take it slow, the day is still long." He looked at them smiled and added, "Celebrate today, be merry, be with your families but remember tomorrow you go on your special sacred mission." He then raised both his hands in the direction of the heavens, signaling that the celebrations should now commence.

As the old High Priest turned around and slowly started walking toward the temple's steep stairs followed by his Acolytes, The twenty-four young men with a smile in their faces and feeling very proud crossed their right arms and politely bowed their heads towards the Sacred Temple. Then turning together as they were taught, bowed in front of the people of Lamanai and in the four directions of the Cardinal Points. They had now officially become men and new citizens of Lamanai. Almost immediately the musical bands and orchestras began playing. People started shouting jubilantly and singing while they danced to the tunes of their favorite bands. Everywhere people were eating and drinking. Some of the men were already getting intoxicated with Balche or other wines and jumped and danced joyously around the plaza.

The High Priest Lord Sac Pek was an old but very wise spiritual leader. He was famous across the allied cities for his ability in prophecy and divinity. Many other high priests came from far and near to consult with him about what course to take when they were suffering a drought or even when there was too much rain for their crops.

Even as a child he had had special powers over other children, he was always the leader, and he was always the one that made the decisions about which games to play. His grandfather and father who had also been high priests saw great things in Sac Pek. So, for that reason they had initiated him at a very early age as a Chilam of Lamanai. At a very early age he had learned to read and write and now he had written several books about divinity and prophecy. Books that were used by other high priests of the sister cities to help teach other upcoming and aspiring young high priests in the ways of the gods and the Maya People.

As the old high priest Sac Pek sat in his room inside the Sacred Temple he could hear the music playing in the plaza below and he could also hear the people shouting and singing merrily. It had been many years since a celebration like this had been held in his city and he felt very content that he was the one who had encouraged the ruler to declare that this day should be celebrated this way. Lord Sac Pek wanted his people to be happy, he loved them very much and he felt that they deserved a day of great celebration. Though he told no one, not even the ruler that hard times were approaching. In a dream he had seen the scourge of wars involving his beloved city. He had also seen droughts and hurricanes destroying cities, in visions, when conducting rituals.

As he once more read a history book that his great grandfather had written a long time ago he could see that his city had been at war many times, even with neighboring cities. This caused much sadness to him for he believed that the gods only loved the people who were peaceful and loving. For that reason and at a very early age as the official Sacred High Priest of Lamanai he began traveling to all the neighboring cities in an effort to unite them. He was a great dynamic orator and people would come from everywhere in the countryside to hear his message of peace. The cities and its people loved him and this caused the rulers to unite and trade with one another. He had been instrumental in creating the Allied Territories and Sister Cities.

Now once more the old man was troubled, thinking about his dreams and visions of war. Who was planning on war? Would it be a surprise attack on his city or would they declare war? Was it a neighboring territory or was it their enemies from the Far North? Was it possible that it would occur when he was still alive? Or would it occur many years after his death? It was hard for him to believe it would be the armies of the far North for they knew about their alliances and they had actually been defeated once in the Battle of Chac'temal. The wise old high priest had no answers for these questions, at least not yet, the reason he chose not to bother anyone about it yet. The army of Lamanai was very well trained and prepared and this kept his heart and mind at ease.

One day, many years ago as the Holy Man was returning from one of his peace mission from the city of Caracol he and his two Chilams accompanying him, came upon a dying female Jaguar and her two cubs. He was very young at that time and was very strong and energetic and he loved and respected all animals. So, immediately with the help of his men, started medically treating the Jaguar but it was useless for the female Jaguar had apparently been seriously injured with a spear and died twenty minutes after the young holy man had found it. Probably it had tried to attack a hunter or traveler who had ventured too close to its young ones and defending himself had struck it with a spear.

A baby Jaguar was dead besides the mother and another was lying besides her trying to get comfort from its dying mother. Young Sac Pek immediately held the baby Jaguar under one arm and began feeding it with bits of dried meat and water. The baby Jaguar, immediately after that, began licking Sac Pek's face lovingly and with appreciation. The young Holy Man then decided to take back the baby Jaguar as a gift to his friend Nohoch Zac Mai the then young prince of Lamanai. Moreover, there could be no way they could leave it there, it would surely die from starvation or maybe even killed by another wild animal. He began calling the baby Jaguar, Spots, after an unusual huge black spot the cub had on its head.

In all the cities that the Holy Men entered along the way to Lamanai they were followed by the robust little Jaguar. People everywhere were amazed in seeing a Holy Man followed by a young Jaguar and this only added more popularity to the already famous dynamic young orator who spoke about peace and how the gods wanted the Maya Territories to live in peace with one another.

Sac Pek had presented the young female Jaguar to his friend Prince Nohoch Zak Mai who was delighted with the playful cat. He kept it as his personal pet for many years until it died of natural causes. The female Jaguar kept in a cage in the balcony of the Royal Palace was actually an offspring of the son of Spots the baby Jaguar the Holy Man had presented to his friend many years ago. After Lord Nohoch Zak Mai ascended to the throne of Lamanai he decided to rename his clan The Royal Jaguar Clan and his personal guards became the Royal Jaguar Order of Soldiers of whom Crocodile Tooth had become its chief.

Two days before the old king of Lamanai, Nohoch Zak Mai's father, passed away, he announced that his oldest son would succeed him as ruler of the Lamanai Provinces. After his passing and a month of mourning, Lord Nohoch Zak Mai, was officially crowned king of the Lamanai Provinces. He then married a very intelligent and beautiful princess from the city of Xunantunich. After two years of being married they were blessed with their first child, a young handsome prince. As the gods would have it, though, the young prince was born with a rare disease and was always too sick to play outside of the palace. It broke the King and Queens heart to see him like this. All the Royal Physicians tried their best to cure him but he only got worse as the days went by. Other rulers from nearby provinces sent their very best physicians and holy men to see to the young prince but all to no avail.

On his eighth birthday the young prince succumbed to his illness. He died early one morning after his mother had personally given him a bath. It was a time of great sadness for the Royal Family and their people. For two months the king could not be seen. He didn't appear anymore on his balcony to wave at his people that always gathered in the royal plaza below. The people were beginning to wonder if they had lost their king along with their prince.

One day, at the end of his second month of grieving, he sent word that the people should gather in the Royal Plaza so he could address them. After his people had gathered in the plaza he assured them that his grieving was over and that he and the queen would go on a journey to one of the islands of Chac'temal for two weeks to pray and meditate. His friend, the High Priest Lord Sac Pek would act as ruler of Lamanai for the days he would be absent.

Ten years after the young prince had died, the beautiful princess Shining Blue Star was born. This brought a lot of happiness to the Royal Family and to all the people of Lamanai. Having no other sibling, she became the sole heir to the provinces of Lamanai. After the death of the young prince, for many years the ruler had tried to convince the queen to bear him another child but she always refused. Every time, before making love, she would drink a tea made from the Wild Yam. This root, found in the rainforest, acted as an anticonceptive and had traditionally been used for hundreds of years by Maya women who didn't want to get pregnant. Having lost her first born made her afraid of conceiving another child. It wasn't until ten years later that she was convinced by the King and the Holy Men that this time, the Goddess of childbirth and medicine Ixchell, had promised to bless them with a healthy child.

Indeed, eleven years after that, it was quite obvious that the young princess had been blessed with an abundance of intelligence, incomparable beauty and good health. In the very near future she would definitely be a great ruler and certainly make a young fortunate prince very happy.

CHAPTER THREE ...

At the *Luum Mak* ceremonies and after the High Priest and his Chilams had retired to their quarters, the Ruler Nohoch Zak Mai stood up and raised his scepter. Immediately, the Sacred Conch Shell could be heard blowing once more, five long melodious tunes. This was the signal for the men to break ranks and for the presentations to begin. The musicians continued playing and immediately the people started shouting and dancing in happiness in seeing acrobats and gymnasts do their magical presentations. On one corner of the plaza surrounded by spectators, were a group of dancers that had been invited from the western city of Caracol for this special occasion. All the dance group members wore brightly colored costumes and their faces were painted with different color paints. They were dancing like in a trance reenacting a victorious battle that had been fought against their city and the city of Tikal many, many, years ago. The spectators were applauding with glee enjoying every moment of the dance and other presentations.

Everywhere along the Sacred Plaza, long tables were filled with fruits, vegetables and meats prepared in a variety of ways. One table was laden with fruits and vegetables some to be eaten raw, others made into jam and sweets while others were simply roasted and salted with sea salt. Papayas, Jicamas, Guavas, Zapotes, Squash, Craboo, Tomatoes, Avocados, Sweet Potatoes, Cohune Nuts, *Hawactes* and many other delicacies were present in huge quantities for the people to enjoy. Another table was laden with meats also prepared in a vast variety. Deer, Turkey, fish, Armadillo, Currassow, Iguanas, Tapir and Peccaries were only some of the game meats prepared by the women, in soups, stews, roasted, and even prepared in Annatto Seed paste, gravy. Another long table still, was full with all kinds of fruit juices, fresh rain water, Palm heart, corn, and *Balche* wines. Pots of fresh Black and Red Beans cooked in every way, was also set on tables.

Most important of all, set on one table for the people to enjoy was "Sun Beams of the Gods" Maize or Corn cooked and prepared in every conceivable way. Bread and *Tamalitos* made from ground young corn, *Atole* or corn porridge sweetened with honey or flavored with vanilla, soft and hard Tamales prepared with a variety of meats, with or without Chili Peppers, Penchuks, Panades, Tacos, Garnaches. Tortillas, boiled and or roasted young corn and the list could go on and on.

Maize constituted a high percentage of the Maya people's diet. A passage in the Popol Vuh, the sacred book of the Maya people also explains how the gods created mankind out of Yellow and White Corn. It was also the first food of the Maya People. The amount of corn stored for future consumption marked the wealth status of all Maya Cities; it was indeed the food of the Gods and the Maya people.

The people of Lamanai and their invited guests hadn't seen such a huge celebration for a long time. The last huge celebration that the people could remember was thirty-five years ago when Nohoch Zak Mai succeeded his father and became ruler of Lamanai.

The last ceremony and celebration this year wasn't half as grandiose as this one. The *Tac'Te* sacred ceremony. That is when; the High Priest and his assistants removed a chain of red shells from around the waist of twelve year old girls, initiating them into puberty age. At this age the girls would also be ready to continue studies like mastering the art of sewing, weaving, cooking, child birth assistance, and healing; among other noble professions. Marrying age for young Maya girls was fourteen years and older. These chains had been placed around young girls waists when they were five years old. For the boys, celebrating their *Luum Mak* today was the beginning of four year training that would lead them to master whatever trade was chosen for them. All the boys were anxious to prove to their ruler, family and people that they were going to be the best at whatever profession destiny had in store for them.

Before the festivities were over, Box Balam and one of his friends he was talking to were approached by a Jaguar Order Guard *Nacom* or war captain, his name was Chacbe. Immediately both boys placed their right thumb on their hearts, bowed their heads and simultaneously greeted him. "At ease men," he said, "I am glad I met you two together because you both have been assigned to me, I will be your mentor on your special mission," He held them both by their shoulders and said, "don't worry it's nothing dangerous, none of you new men will go on a dangerous mission as of yet. Your mission," he continued, "is to bring ten bags of sea salt from the Eastern Great Waters to Lamanai, I will be accompanying you all the way, but," he added, "you will be responsible to gather or hunt your own food going and coming back if necessary, for this is also part of your training."

The two boys glanced around and saw other guards talking to other colleagues of theirs. The notion that not only they would be going on such a rigorous journey put them at ease. The Royal Guard continued saying. 'You will be in charge of the map that will take us through the territories of Altun Ha and then to the Great Open Waters; in other words you will be doing everything on your own as you were taught or trained to do, I am only to help you if necessary or if there is an emergency," Chacbe looked into the boys eyes and asked, "are we all clear on this?" "yes" answered both boys in unison.

Box Balam knew about Chacbe he was a legendary warrior and his brother, Big Tapir, always spoke very highly of him. He also knew that as warrior chief his brother would not accompany any of the new men but Box guessed that his brother must have recommended that Chacbe be purposely appointed mentor to Box and his companion and for that he was very thankful. Of all the guards, there couldn't be a better one than Chacbe to be his mentor.

His friend accompanying him on this mission was Red Cat. He was also an excellent ball player and he also longed to play in the Royal Team, he lived in a courtyard near Box's one and Box had always played ball against his team. He was very pleased that he was the one accompanying him. Red Cat's father was from Altun Ha he had married a girl from Lamanai and had chosen to make his home here. Red Cat belonged to the 'Green Iguana Clan' a clan from Red Cat's mothers' family. They were renowned to be talented and great farmers. Red Cat's father was a prosperous farmer who was loved and respected throughout Lamanai, Altun Ha and Hol'patin. He was always generous and kind to people who had come from far away to purchase or trade with his agricultural products.

Unlike Box, who had never been to Altun Ha, Red Cat had been their twice the recent years. He had been taken there by his father to visit his grandparents and other relatives. He loved to tell his friends about his adventures while swimming or fishing in the Great Waters of the East with his grandfather and cousins. They loved to go fishing on his grandfather's huge dugout canoe. The Great Waters was a mere nine miles away east of the city of Altun Ha and the people of Altun Ha were known to be great fishermen and seafarer traders. They also cultivated salt in small quantities but most of their salt, and that of other cities, came from cities of the far North.

"You will love the sea, Box," Red Cat said after being dismissed by Chacbe and as they walked towards their homes to rest and be ready for the next day. "It is so huge their seems to be no end to it you will love swimming in it too; I hope we can make a stop at Altun Ha," he added, "I would love to see my grandparents once more, you would really love it there Box; It's a really beautiful city." Box Balam felt lucky that his companion would be someone who knew about the Great Waters. Before he went to sleep he offered praises to the gods that their mission be accomplished safely and on time.

The people around the city were all talking about the various missions assigned to the young men. Everybody acknowledged the fact that even though this had never been done before, these missions would be a great opportunity for the young men to travel and meet people from other Maya cities. Many of them had never been beyond the borders of Lamanai, and unless they were appointed soldiers, ambassadors or become traveling merchants they might never have another opportunity to do so. Mainly because of the tension that was growing between the territories of the Far North and the Allied Cities once more. The Rulers of the allied cities, for the past year now, have been hearing rumors that the armies of the Far North were in extensive training. No word had come that they were actually preparing for war, but the rulers of the Allied Cities trusted them not. They were a savage people who had to be constantly monitored.

Some of the new men would be traveling south all the way to the Motagua valley to bring raw Jade to Lamanai. Others will be going to the volcanic regions to trade for Obsidian Rocks while others would be going deep in the mountains of the rain forest to collect Quetzal, Toucan, Macaws, and Currassow feathers. Another group had the sacred mission of trapping and bringing back Jaguar and Ocelot skins. Other groups were in charge of the less dangerous but equally important mission of taking gifts like honey, tobacco, mineral and vegetable dyes, Tobacco, vanilla, rubber, and cotton textiles to the rulers of friendly and allied cities like Xunantunich, Cahal Pech, Caracol, Las Milpas and Noh Mul.

The intention was to cement the good sisterhood relations they now enjoyed. The artisans of Lamanai were famous for their beautiful Polychrome Vases and plates; some of these would be presented as gifts to the rulers of the sister cities of Lamanai. The scribes of Lamanai were also famous for producing some of the best books in the region made from the bark of the Wild Fig Tree. Some of these will also be presented to the rulers, some of them blank and some of them explaining the recent accomplishment of the people of Lamanai. All of them would also be taking Cacao Beans, which constituted the principal currency for the Maya, with them, in order to trade with the Royal Families. This was a most sought after commodity by the Royal Families who would be making it into the precious and delicious Chocolate Drink.

CHAPTER FOUR ....

'We'll be leaving our canoe at that dock, yonder," Chacbe said to his two new recruits as he pointed to a small wooden dock almost concealed in the bushes on the banks of the lagoon. Box and Red Cat expertly guided their small dugout canoe to where Chacbe was pointing. "We leave our canoe here then we proceed on foot men," he said. They had been paddling their canoe on the lagoon for over an hour now and the boys were only too happy to be able to be on firm land and continue their journey.

After securing their canoe, they once more checked their equipment. An Obsidian knife in a sheath around their waist, a sling with a pouch of small rounded pebbles, a long spear with a sharp pointed flint spearhead and their bows and quiver of thirteen arrows given to them by the High Priest, their most prized possessions. They made sure that these items were in complete order. These weapons were of extreme importance every time someone would go on a journey. You could never be too cautious when traveling through the jungle. A frightened or injured animal could kill you very easily. The most feared one was the Yellow Jawed snake which was known to kill a man with one strike in minutes. The sling and pebbles was used to hunt small game like birds, rabbits and armadillos and the spear and bow and arrow was used for hunting bigger animals like deer and tapir. They had also been reminded many times, though, to always be very respectful to all living things. A man should never kill an animal if it was not for consumption. The gods always looked upon and took care of its creatures.

In a deerskin bag slung across their back with a strap across their forehead that they called a *Mekapal,* were their sleeping equipment, their cooking and eating utensils, drinking water kept cool in a calabash gourd and gifts for Lord Choc Chen the Ruler of Altun Ha. They followed silently behind their mentor looking everywhere and always prepared to face danger as they were taught while growing up.

"The jungle," his uncle Crocodile Tooth always said to him when he was out hunting with him one day, "can be your best friend but it can also be your worst enemy it will feed you, heal you and give you shelter and water but, it can also kill you if you don't respect it; always beware and respect its rightful owners the wild animals specially the sacred Jaguar for whom our Rulers' Clan has been named, remember," he always said, "most diseases come from the jungle so always beware and always be clean."

It was as if Box was hearing these words whispered in his ears by his great warrior uncle. "I remember uncle," he said silently to himself. Tradition mandated that every time an animal of the forest was killed, be it for food or even because it posed a threat to someone, a bit of its blood always be thrown in the direction of the four winds of the world in respect to the other animals. The same was true when clearing the forest to make a milpa or for any other reason, a special prayer always had to be said to the gods and keepers of the jungle. This tradition was recorded in the sacred books written hundreds of years ago. A tradition expected to be followed by everyone going through the rain forests or jungles of the Maya people.

The path being taken by the three men today was used extensively by merchants who traveled everywhere trading their goods. From small islands and the coast they would bring dried fish, salt, and Stingray spines for ritual bloodletting and seashells. From the inland cities they would take Jaguar skins, exotic birds' plumage, Jade, Obsidian and pottery. This was also the same route that the army of Lamanai had marched through, to join forces with the army of Altun Ha, then to Chac'temal to help them fight the army of the Far North. Chacbe was still a young boy when this battle occurred, but he remembered it very well, though. All the preparations that had to be done to prepare the army and to protect Lamanai if enemy troops infiltrated the area was still vivid in his mind. How will he ever forget how is mother cried when his father didn't come back from the war.

When news had arrived in Chac'temal, which was also a port city that a huge army was coming by way of the great waters. They immediately sent emmissaries to their sister cities to summon for help. Three thousand soldiers laid in wait for the armies of the Far North. One thousand soldiers waited on the beach and two thousand came from behind the enemy. The Northern armies upon arriving in Chac'temal waters and seeing only a few of their soldiers on the beach thought that they had surprised Chac'temal, and that their allied armies had not yet arrived. This cost them dearly because over one thousand soldiers led by Crocodile Tooth were hiding inside the thick mangroves, near Cerros, in their long canoes waiting in ambush.

When Chief Crocodile Tooth gave the orders, five hundred men led by Chacbe's father attacked on the right flank with spears raining down on the enemy and five hundred men led by Crocodile Tooth's brother attacked with hundreds of arrows raining down on the army of the Far North. The friendly forces on the beach, led by Great Mot Mot by that time had jumped in their canoes and armed with *Maquahuills,*—war clubs—and *Atlatles,*—spear thrower-, attacked the enemy from the front. It was a fierce battle and even though the enemy had lost many men in the first two attacks they were determined not to retreat, their chief and captain urged them to keep on fighting. The hand to hand combat was fierce and the armies of the North were also great warriors but when their chief realized that they were outnumbered two to one and after suffering so many casualties on the surprise attack, he ordered the retreat conch shell horn be blown. The battle took over four hours before the enemy retreated in defeated.

Hundreds of soldiers on both sides had died but the ruler of Chac'temal and the chiefs of the allied forces knew that they had won the battle and possibly the war. It was decided not to pursue the fleeing enemy and kill them since they had fought bravely, moreover they wanted them to go back home defeated and take back word about the allied forces great army. The surprise attack was an ingenious military tactic engineered by the great warrior chief of the Jaguar Order of Soldiers and Army of Lamanai, Chief Crocodile Tooth.

As the battle was going on, Red Cloud, the ruler's brother, who was ordered to defend the Royal Palace if necessary, was looking at all this with displeasure from atop the highest point of the Royal Palace. Unknowingly to his brother Great Mot Mot, he had been secretly consorting with spies of the North to help him overthrow Great Mot Mot so he could become ruler and after him, his son. Years ago when his brother would conceive only girls he was quite sure that he would inherit the throne of Chac'temal and its empire as was mandated by tradition and he had been happy. Then, a son was born to the aging ruler and he named him Great Macaw.

Red Cloud was ten years younger than Great Mot Mot and his future looked promising but then Great Macaw was born and unless the great ruler died before his son became thirteen years old, he would never become ruler. He longed for the death of either his brother or his son. His hatred for his brother and his son was so great that he started plotting secretly against them and after consorting with enemy spies and with the promise that they would help him become ruler, he fed them with information about the city's defenses. "Our ruler only wants an opportunity to trade with your rich empire," the spies had lied to him. They never told him that their aim was to conquer Chac'temal and after that, the cities of Noh Mul and Holpatin. Great Mot Mot, though, had been suspecting his brother as a traitor for some time now so he never mentioned to him that friendly forces were coming to help him. By the time Red Cloud realized that an ambush had been sprung on the army who was suppose to crown him new ruler of Chac'temal, it was too late for him to warn them. His hatred towards his brother became even more. So, he continued to plan how he could kill his brother.

After the great battle, Chief Crocodile Tooth and his two captains, his brother and Chacbe's father, and some of his most trusted Jaguar Order soldiers decided to camp in a heavily wooded area near the city, while the rest of his soldiers rested inside the city. Great Mot Mot had told him about his suspicion of Red Cloud and he and his high priest were deliberating on what to do about him. Five miles surrounding the city were fresh well rested soldiers guarding the city with their runners ready to contact the rest of the troops if the enemy decided to make a counter attack. Even though, the chiefs thought it was very unlikely, for the enemy had suffered too many casualties. At the thought of friendly soldiers surrounding their area Chief Crocodile Tooth and his men, being very tired after the victorious battle, decided to relax and get some well deserved rest.

At three in the morning, after killing his guard on duty, they were attacked by soldiers loyal to Red Cloud. Red Cloud thought that by eliminating Crocodile Tooth and his captains he stood a better chance of one day eliminating his brother. Crocodile Tooth and his *Nacoms* or captains almost never slept soundly and they always had their weapons at hand. At the first cry they woke up swinging their *maquahuills* at their attackers. It was very bad for they were outnumbered and Crocodile Tooth saw his men fall dead one by one including his captains, his brother and one of his cousins.

He himself had suffered a big chop wound on his left shoulder and a broken spear was protruding from his right leg. As he fell to the ground and being left for dead in the darkness as the attackers fled, he recognized one of them as a guard to Red Clouds palace. Ten minutes after the surprise attack, friendly soldiers patrolling the area came to their aid; it was too late, though. They were appalled at the massacre that lay in front of them. Most of the Royal Jaguar Soldiers accompanying Crocodile Tooth, including

Chacbe's father were dead, but they found Chief Crocodile Tooth and two other soldiers still breathing, they also found four dead soldiers belonging to Red Clouds personal guard. Immediately a search was conducted and Red Cloud, his family and all his guards were arrested.

Early the next day, at the crack of dawn, seven of the guards arrested were executed in the middle of the Sacred Plaza. Five more of the captives had been stripped of their clothing and their bodies were completely painted in blue, and were kept in a cell inside the temple. These ones were destined to be sacrificed to the gods. In a cell inside the palace were Red Cloud and his family waiting for a decision by the council of high priests of the sister cities, on Red Clouds fate.

It was almost three weeks before Chief Crocodile Tooth was fit enough to return home. The death of his men lay heavy on his shoulders, he blamed himself, he knew about Red Cloud yet he had allowed himself to be too trusting. He had been given a huge hero celebration before he left Chac'temal and when he arrived in Lamanai, but that did very little to appease his guilty feeling.

Many years ago when Box was very little he had heard stories about how soldiers had to accompany merchants to one city then soldiers from that city would accompany them to another city to protect them from raiding parties belonging to the Far North; But since the last battle against the foreign army of the North when they tried to invade Chac'temal, and where they suffered huge casualties, they hadn't been seen since. Yes, there have been robbers and raiding parties but they were believed to be renegades and malcontents of neighboring cities. It was fortunate that for many years now there had been peace for the Maya People sister cities.

There were also rumors that robbers had come in groups near the borders of the Chac'temal's empire to steal their Cacao beans left to dry on the sun. There was no evidence though, that they belonged to the Northern Empire. The new young ruler of Chac'temal, Great Macaw, had managed to keep the robbers at bay. He had a well organized unit of trusted soldiers who responded only to Great Macaw himself. They were trained in the tactics of attack and hide and search and rescue by a captain of the famous Tactical Jaguar Order of Soldiers from Lamanai. They were the ones in charge of keeping the robbers at bay. The young ruler tried not to think about his uncle Red Cloud ever trying something against him or his people. Actually, he even thought, that like his father, he was probably long dead. He would never believe how wrong he was.

THE NORTHERN TERRITORIES

PEOPLE OF THE CLOUD SERPENT CLAN

CHAPTER FIVE ⸺

"This is the right time my lords," Red cloud said, as he kneeled on one foot looking down, addressing the Ruler and High Priest of the city of the Far North, "my brother has been dead for a long time," he reminded them, "and his son is too young and stupid to rule Chac'temal and its people, me or my son who is now of age are the rightful rulers of Chac'temal." The ruler, Lord *Tepocoatle* and his High Priest were today holding a special meeting with Red Cloud because, for the past nine months he had been begging for it.

"Tell me Red Cloud." said the High Priest of the Cloud Serpent Clan, "why should we give you our soldiers to fight for you? Have you forgotten how many good soldiers we lost the last time we tried to invade Chac'temal so we could declare you ruler of that city? We have been at peace with the Southern Cities for years now. What makes you think that you can now conquer them and be the new ruler of Chac'temal? Haven't our emissaries informed you of their alliance with other great cities like Lamanai and Caracol?

Tell me, please Red Cloud," he said, as he stood up shaking his long ceremonial staff, as his long ceremonial headdress of colorful bird feathers moved from left to right as a gust of wind blew in from the East.

"My Lords," answered Red cloud, "these people are weak, they no longer have the great warriors they once had, their rulers are weak, they dedicate themselves only in building more temples and planting more corn. They are constantly celebrating and getting drunk with *Balche*. My spies reported that they no longer care to continue expanding, and training their armies extensively as we do".

Red Cloud crossed his right hand across his chest and bowed even lower "my Lords," he said, "all these years you have given me and my family refuge and protection and for that we are forever grateful. We still love it here, but, I also come from a Royal Family as you all know. I was driven out by my brother because I believed in you and your ways in ruling a city as I continue to do today, I beg of you oh mighty ruler", he implored, "that you give me the opportunity to capture back my rightful place in Chac'temal, only then we can together conquer Holpatin, Altun Ha, Noh Mul and even Lamanai." "For years my Lords," he continued, "I have sent spies everywhere in the deep South, I have also sent warrior parties to Chac'temal to rob their Cacao Beans of which I have presented to you every time. I am ready, my son Nohoch Pek is ready and my faithful warriors are ready," he pleaded.

"With you on my side we can conquer the Southern Territories and bring them under our command one by one," he concluded.

Having heard all this, the ruler Lord *Tepocoatle* stood up, the sign that Red Cloud was being dismissed. "We have heard you Red Cloud and we understand your situation but this is a very delicate matter and it must be discussed very carefully with our war chiefs and council of elders," said Lord *Tepocoatle*. "As from this time you will send no more raiding parties or spies to the Southern Cities, is that understood Red Cloud". The ruler said as he started walking towards the entrance of another room of the Royal Palace. "You will be summoned back in five days where then we will give you an answer".

"Yes my Lords", answered Red Cloud as he stood up and walked towards and down the steep steps of the Royal Palace of the Cloud Serpent Clan with high hopes in his heart. He walked with even higher spirits towards his family's house where his son Nohoch Pek and leaders of a mercenary group he had hired along with his faithful guards, were waiting to hear about the outcome of the meeting with *Tepocoatle* and the High Priest.

After briefing them, Red Cloud and his son Nohoch Pek, walked towards the edge of the sacred plaza where a shrine had been erected to honor the fallen warriors in the last war against Chac'temal and her Allied Cities.

"Soon, very soon my son," he told Nohock Pek. We will be the rulers of the land of our forefathers. We will once again be able to go to our islands to fish and swim as we did when you were little and with the help of Lord *Tepocoatle* we will have all the southern territories under our control. We will reign over them, but," said Red Cloud as he looked straight into Nohock Pek's dark brown eyes. "You will once more head south this time, not to Chac'temal but to Lamanai, you will take only five of your best warriors with you. You will go by the sea and not by the rivers." Red Cloud then explained that he was to go and find Crocodile Tooth and kill him.

He never forgot that Crocodile Tooth was the one responsible for his failed attempt in killing his brother and becoming ruler. His spies had already told him that Crocodile Tooth was alive and well. He was retired from the army so he would some days spend hours alone on his garden. "You will bring back nothing, but the Jade pendant he wears around his neck awarded to him by Great Mot Mot after our shameful expulsion from our city. That will be the sign that you have killed him," he whispered to Nohoch Pek.

"When you come back", he continued, "The armies of the Cloud Serpent Clan will be almost ready to invade Chac'temal. Now get your men ready for at sunrise tomorrow you depart," he concluded. "Remember Nohoch Pek, my son, this is a top secret mission, nobody must know that you are headed to Lamanai. We must not jeopardize our military campaign against the Allied Cities."

It was that time of year when the Southern Lowlands abounded with wild fruit. So, Chacbe and his two companions usually stopped to snack on Black Berries *Hawacte*, wild *Craboo*, *Zapotes* and even *Mammees* and wild Papayas. Their favorite though, was the heart of the young palm tree. The two boys also enjoyed very much cutting Water Vines and letting its sweet water trickle down their throats to quench their thirst after a stifling, hot and humid day through the rainforest.

At a very young age, the two boys, and the same could be said for most boys of the Maya People, had learned the ways of the jungle. They learned to recognize different medicinal plants, edible fruits and the poisonous ones as well. They could recognize and made sure that they always stayed away from the dreaded and highly toxic Poisonwood tree. The

Poisonwood tree released a dark looking resin that when exposed to human skin created a high degree of burn. As Mother Nature would have it though, there was a tree that always grew near the toxic trees known as the Gumbolimbo tree. The resin of this tree was the antidote for this dreaded toxic tree. It didn't make the burn disappear but it cooled the burn allowing it to heal faster. It was always wise to stay away from the dreaded Poisonwood tree, though. They also learned to imitate the calls of certain birds good for consumption and they knew when to stay away from certain wild animals. So, Chacbe was very happy he was assigned to two very bright boys. This made his job a lot easier.

About four in the evening that day, while the two other men rested, Box began cutting the bark of a large Sapodilla tree trunk to extract its resin to make chewing gum. The tree was loaded with its sweet fruit and high above on the tallest branch a flock of eight Scarlet Macaws were noisily having a feast with the ripe fruit. A little bit lower on another branch was a flock of small green and red parrots also noisily pecking at the ripe Sapodilla fruit. Scattered everywhere around the tree were half eaten fruit dropped by the greedy birds. As Box looked around he thought he saw movement deep in the forest behind some trees and a strange sensation crept over him just like when he was washing by his clan's artificial pond yesterday morning. The feeling you get like when someone is looking at you, yet you see no one.

He looked carefully in the area where he thought he saw the movement but saw nothing more than trees, shrubs and the occasional bird jumping from one limb to the next. He was about to tell his friends but dismissed it as it being just a wild animal looking for food and trying to stay away from them. He had heard stories from elders about a mythological creature called the *Tata Duende*, the dwarf evil keeper of the jungle who tricked people to get lost and later killed them. Or even the *Xtabai*, a beautiful maiden, actually an evil spirit of the jungle, with long shiny black hair who lured young handsome men to their domain, then kill them. Many of the old people believed in these creatures and some actually swear in having had encounters with them, but not Box Balam and he was not going to start believing now. He would dare not mention it to his mentor and friend, less he wanted to be teased or ridiculed in believing in mythological stories. So, he decided to leave his suspicions aside and prepare a fire to make *chicle, chewing gum.*

"We must hurry", Chacbe called, "if we want to be in Altun Ha before it gets too dark". Both young men put their fire out after boiling the sap from the Sappodilla Tree to a thick consistency mixed with vanilla for taste. Red Cat and Box then gathered a few of the Sapodilla fruits for later consumption. After the Chicle, cooled they put a wad in their mouth and hurried behind Chacbe.

"Today," Said Chacbe, "you learn jungle survival skills, how to eat and live from the jungle but you must also learn how to fight in the jungle. In close quarter battle or when you are attacked in the thick jungle your bow and arrows become almost useless." He continued by saying, "you need to become expert fighters in using the *Maquahuil* your spear and your knife in the jungle. The bows and arrows will only become very useful in an open field combat and when fighting in the open waters, Remember all this, for when we return to Lamanai you begin your real military training it doesn't matter which profession you are appointed to after that. Remember; always keep your weapons ready for they come first not your food".

Some weapons were new for the Maya warriors. They had reproduced it from some left by warriors of the Far North after the famous battle at Chac'temal.

As they continued heading towards the city of Altun Ha and then the great open sea after that, Box couldn't help thinking about the movement he saw and the strange sensation he had felt earlier. He was about to tell Red Cat when Chacbe announced, "in about thirty minutes we should be entering the city so, look smart and be proud for today we are ambassadors of our great Lamanai". The two boys were expecting this. For the past couple of hours they had been passing through milpas and had waved at the occasional farmer hard at work in his field. They had suspected that they couldn't be too far away. Years ago, Red Cat had been through here but he didn't remember it quite well. They had come through almost three miles of Sacbeob. On both sides of the causeway were crisscrossed raised agricultural fields filled with corn stalks and other vegetables.

It was almost dark when the men arrived in the outskirts of the city of Altun Ha. Kinich Ahau, the sun god, was already in his journey through the nine chambers of the underworld—nighttime—fighting the demons just to appear victorious the next day and continue blessing the world with its light.

From a distance the three men of Lamanai could see a huge plume of smoke coming from a huge conch shell made from clay from atop a tall altar. "The Sacred Smoking Conch Shell," said Chacbe very surprised. "The sign of a grieving city, what could have happened?" Box and Red Cat had never heard about a smoking conch shell so they didn't know what to say. They only stood admiring the beautiful city. There were flowering trees and shrubs everywhere their sweet smell mingling with the unmistakable sweet aroma of burning Copal Incense. "The city is even more beautiful than the last time I was here," Red Cat whispered to Box.

As they approached the city even closer, a group of royal soldiers came towards them.

"Greetings and may the peace of the gods guide you always," said Chacbe reciting the greetings of soldiers to one another". The three men politely raising their open left hand in the direction of the Royal Soldiers who had come to greet them. "Welcome to Altun Ha and may the gods always guide you too," responded the leader of the group.

"We are here, on a mission for our ruler Lord Nohoch Zak Mai on training for these two young men, "explained Chacbe, "We also bring a message of peace and gifts to your great ruler Lord Choc Chen.

"Yes," answered the lead soldier, "but first you will be escorted to where you can wash, eat then rest. Tonight you are our guests and a hut will be prepared for you. We were expecting you, a farmer had sent his son to inform us of your presence in the neighborhood they had recognized you as travelers from Lamanai, so, please take your rest, tomorrow you will be able to present your message and gifts to our ruler. I am sure he will have a word of caution to you and a message to take back to your ruler."

When they walked around a huge plaza surrounded with a beautifully painted residential complex Box could see that, like Lamanai, Altun Ha was a beautiful and prosperous wealthy city. The gardens adjacent to the residences and homes were filled with many varieties of vegetables. Residential homes and palaces belonging to the Royal Families had beautiful, colorful flowers planted everywhere around it. Leading to the top of the Sacred Temple, on each step, were huge painted clay pots. Some of them having dates that went back hundreds of years, exotic Bromeliads and Orchids were growing on old wood in some of the painted pots.

As they were led by an escort towards the Ambassadorial Plaza to a hut belonging to the Ambassador of Lamanai where they would be staying for the night, they passed through a small menagerie of animals. There were several Spider Monkeys who chirped noisily at them while hanging by their tails from the branch of a huge tree. A Black Jaguar patrolled his enclosure majestically, paying no attention to the men passing by. Kinkajous, Ocelots, Pumas, Black Howler Monkeys, Morelets crocodiles and a Three Toed Sloth making its long and very slow journey to the top of a tree; were only a few of the animals kept at the zoo. On one side of the menagerie a huge collection of birds were kept.

Beautiful birds that looked like sparkling jewels decorating the tree limbs they were perching on. Colorful Toucan birds, majestic Scarlet Macaws, sacred Quetzal birds, White and Yellow Head parrots were only some of the birds chirping and singing excitedly as the men walked past their enclosures.

Far beyond the menagerie the biggest majestic Sacred Temple of Altun Ha dedicated to the Sun God Kinich Ahau could be seen. Its ceremonial plaza surrounded with smaller temples dedicated to other gods. The Majestic Sacred Temple was famous around the Maya provinces and cities. Its construction was started two hundred years ago by the great grandfather of Lord Choc Chen. Since then every new king has changed or added to its beautiful architecture. The temple was not the biggest in the area but it certainly was the most sacred. Rulers, high priests, ambassadors, royalty and peasants alike came with porters bearing gifts from as far away as Tikal, Copan and Piedras Neagras to pay homage in the temple of the great Kinich Ahau. They come to witness the greatest and most sacred ceremonies and rituals dedicated to Kinich Ahau. Rituals and ceremonies conducted by the high priests of Lamanai and Altun Ha every year.

A huge sculptured head of Kinich Ahau made from the most valuable shiny green Jade was resting on an altar at the very top of the Sacred Temple. This was the biggest carved jade head of Kinich Ahau for hundreds of miles around. This was the representation of the Sun God. Nine animals, a captive enemy warrior and a young virgin maiden were sacrificed to him every year.

CHAPTER SIX ⸱

It was a restless night for the three men visiting Altun Ha, whatever had happened must have been very serious for the ruler Lord Choc Chen to want to have an audience with the Nacom Chacbe. Early the next day two Royal Guards escorted Chacbe to the Royal Palace.

"A few days ago," Lord Choc Chen was saying to Chacbe after welcoming him and his two men to his city. "My eldest son Zac Chen was killed while on a trading mission with a group of merchants to Holpatin. They were ambushed by a group of robbers," he continued, "ten miles down the Dzuluinicob River on the White Crocodile's curve." Chacbe knew the curve on the river, it was legendary, it was a part of the territory of a huge albino crocodile that was considered sacred by the people of Holpatin and Chacbe had actually seen it two times, years ago. "for many months we have been getting reports of renegades stealing Cacao beans from the *Chultuns* of the Chac'temal people," Lord Choc Chen continued saying, "all of this time the Royal

Guards of Chac'temal thought that it was the work of common local thieves; But most recently they have robbed other merchants and because of the tactics they are using the guards began suspecting that it could be the work of a highly trained group of soldiers; the reason they haven't been able to apprehend them. For some time now they were rightly suspecting that they could be mercenary soldiers from the far North Provinces."

Lord Choc Chen looked at Chacbe with very sad eyes and continued saying, "one of our merchants that actually survived the murderous attack on his traveling party managed to recognize one of the marauders as being Nohoch Pek, the now grown son of Red Cloud the exiled uncle of Great Macaw ruler of Chac'temal. All of this time it was the men of Red Cloud who had been sent to rob and wreak havoc in our sister city Chac'temal and neighboring villages. What they were doing so far into our territories still has me puzzled but I am suspecting that they are gathering information about our defenses. The reports are that a group of hunters from Holpatin had found the murdered party of merchants and the only one left alive was found wandering badly injured and lost in the nearby forest. My son and the others were found in their boats, dead, floating downriver. We have brought them back for burial and my son was laid to rest only yesterday but the injured merchant is still in Holpatin recuperating from his injuries.". The old ruler of Altun Ha signaled one of his attendants to bring some chocolate drink for himself, his high priest and Chacbe then continued relating the details of how his son was killed. An envoy had come to Altun Ha from Holpatin with the sad news. The surviving merchant had managed to explain the ordeal while being treated in Holpatin.

He explained that after canoeing down the Dzuluinicob River on the White Crocodile's curve, that fatal day, the merchant leader was about to give the signal to setup camp for the night on the west banks of the river when they came across old tree logs and branches tied together across the river. When the head merchant realized that this was not normal and it might be the work of robbers, he shouted orders to turn back and head for a small, almost concealed tributary of the great river they had seen minutes before, but it was too late since another set of logs had already been towed across the river behind them.

Suddenly war cries had come from the robbers who had their canoes well camouflaged in the nearby mangroves. The young prince and the merchants didn't stand a chance against these robbers who also had weapons that were unmistakably military. It was pure luck then that Ical, one of the merchants, who was only wounded in the right shoulder and his right leg, had let himself float down the river as if dead. He had recognized Nicte, one of Red Clouds treacherous personal guards that had escaped from Chac'temal after red Cloud was arrested. Even with their faces painted black Ical still recognized Nicte as the chief of the group and he was almost sure that one of the young robbers was Nohoch Pek even with his face painted black.

The old ruler took another sip of his hot chocolate drink and said, "Nacom Chacbe, we now know that it was Red Clouds agents who had been robbing all these years and the ones who killed my son. According to Ical one of the older merchants had also recognized Nicte and had told him so. That was the reason we believe, that they decided to slaughter them all even though they probably only wanted to steal their food and jewelry. They probably didn't want to alert the sister cities as to whom they really were." The old ruler clenched his left fist as he continued saying, "Ical swears on Kinich Ahau that it was Nicte and Nohoch Pek and we believe him because, like the old merchant that had told Nicte that he knows him, he had traded extensively with the people of Chac'temal and the family of Red Cloud years back before he became a traitor."

"This can only mean," said Lord Choc Chen that all of this time the Northern Cities have been sending not only robbers but spies to gather information about our defenses. I believe that they must be planning an all scale invasion to Chac'temal headed by Red Cloud. We must immediately put our armies in a state of readiness and be prepared to join forces with our allied city Chac'temal.This is the message you must take back to Lord Nohoch Zak Mai, your ruler. Before you arrived yesterday I had also briefed your ambassador residing here and upon hearing of your arrival here he has agreed that you go back immediately with our message. I have been informed of your mission," he said, "and I believe it's no longer safe for you to go to the great waters for salt I will be sending porters with salt for your ruler as a gift for him and please tell him how much we appreciate the gifts he has sent us. Five of my Royal Guards will also be escorting you back to Lamanai." As the ruler of Altun Ha stood up, a signal that his audience with Chacbe was over, he added, "I understand that the son of a son of Altun Ha is here with us, please permit him to visit with his relatives and family today. Tomorrow you travel back to Lamanai; today you join us in mourning my beloved son Zac Chen who is right now wandering through the nine chambers of the underworld to be united with his ancestors in heaven with our gods."

Chacbe bowed deeply as the ruler and high priest headed towards their chambers and to their families to continue mourning the passing of the beloved prince Zac Chen. He walked down the steep stairs of the Royal Palace, deep in thought, to the courtyard below where his men were waiting. About two hundred people were gathered around the courtyard chanting and crying silently, during the day the mourners would cry silently and at night they would wail and cry loudly. An orchestra was in the middle of the courtyard playing very sad and melancholic music. These people had been mourning here since the dead prince was brought home he had been told. Many people took turns to go home to eat and rest making sure there were always about a hundred people mourning in the courtyard any given time. The people commented on how every time they would see the young prince, Zac Chen, sharing nuts and candies with the peasant children, and almost every day he could be seen by the zoo. He specially loved the spider monkeys. The people of Altun Ha had loved him dearly.

After briefing his men about the outcome of his meeting with Lord Choc Chen; Red Cat was granted permission to go visit his families who lived in a courtyard beyond the Sacred Temple of Kinich Ahau. As Box and Chacbe walked on a causeway that led to their ambassador's residence Box told Chacbe what he saw and the strange feeling he had both in Lamanai and when coming to Altun Ha. "You have been very alert Box and that is a good quality in being a good soldier and in being a good Pok-A-Tok player," He said, "I strongly suspect that what you saw were movements from Red Clouds spies. We must be very careful and alert when we go back."

"Your brother chief Big Tapir and your uncle Crocodile Tooth have told me about your desire in wanting to play ball with the Royal Team" he said to Box while holding him on his right shoulder. "Like them I also believe that you can be an excellent addition to our team. Your uncle Crocodile Tooth was an excellent ball player and I believe you can be too. So Box, I wish you a lot of luck and I pray that you are selected by our high priest." He clapped his hands by his ears at a mosquito while he said, "I will also take it upon myself to tell you about the ceremonial games that children were never allowed to see."

As they approached their hut, in the distance, they could see the huge plume of smoke coming from the huge Sacred Smoking Conch Shell. This was a grim reminder of a people mourning a beloved leader.

As Chacbe rested on his hammock that night, he remembered how years ago his own family had mourned the death of his father. "These men that killed the young prince could very well be some of the ones responsible for my father's death," thought Chacbe.

Many years had gone by since his father was assassinated by Red Cloud's guards at Chac'temal. His father was one of Crocodile Tooth's captains that had been killed while resting in the outskirts of Chac'temal after the Great War that drove back the Armies of the Far North. Chacbe was still a child when the last Great War occurred but he had a vivid memory about his father's burial. He never forgot the sadness and grief he had seen on his mother's face. He remembered his grandmother and all his relatives mourning for many months. He remembered his mother saying that the son of Red Cloud, Nohoch Pek, was about his same age when the war had occurred.

As he grew older, he had then learned that his father had not died in the actual battle of Chac'temal, but had been murdered by some of the same people he had gone to defend. This had been very traumatic for young Chacbe at the time but he overcame it after he was initiated into military school. After he became a fully trained soldier he became obsessed with the idea of finding Red Cloud and to kill him in revenge to his father's death. He vowed to locate the three guards that had escaped from Chactemal after attacking Chief Crocodile Tooth's command post. He knew that some of Red cloud's guards had been executed or sacrificed to the gods but three of them had escaped and one of them was Nicte. He also knew that they had been reunited with Red Clouds family that had been exiled from the Chac'temal territories and were now living in the Far North serving the traitor brother of the ruler of the Chac'temal provinces.

He longed to make a journey to the Far North someday to find and kill these men. He had taken upon himself to learn the strange customs and ways of these people. For months he had questioned an old prisoner of war from the Northern Cities who had been spared from death and was now a slave to the Royal Family. He spent many hours with the old man learning his language, his mannerism and the history of his people. In a few short months he had learned everything there was to be learned about the people of the Far North. All this knowledge would certainly come in handy if he was to one day travel to the city of the Far North to avenge his father.

One day he and his section of six men were assigned to escort and protect if necessary, a group of wealthy merchants on a trading mission to Holpatin, Noh Mul and Chac'temal. As they canoed down river they came upon a strange white juvenile crocodile resting under the shade of a tree surrounded by thick bushes, on the west bank of the river. The merchants and the soldiers alike were amazed at this creature for there were many crocodiles in their lagoons but none like this one.

After spending a night in Holpatin they had learned from an elder that the white crocodile was actually an albino and that they considered it a sacred animal. Everybody was expected to protect and respect this crocodile. This albino crocodile was unique in the sense that unlike other crocodiles it did not bask in the sun; because of its delicate skin it had to constantly be protected from direct sunlight. So, it was always hard to spot it since it was always in the water and when on the banks always hiding between bushes. So, it was always a rare treat when people saw it. The people who came upon it had to bow before it utter a prayer and leave some food for it. Those were the orders of the High Priest of Holpatin.

Upon arriving in Chactemal and were well rested, the merchants then opened their shops to the public. They were to be there for ten days trading with the people of Chac'temal where then they would return to Lamanai with goods acquired in the cities they had visited; always accompanied by the soldiers who were to protect them from robbers along the way. Chacbe thought that ten days was a perfect opportunity for him to travel to the Far North and try to locate Red Cloud and Nicte. He had instructed three of his men to stay in Chac'temal with the merchants and three of them to accompany him.

After changing from military clothes to civilian clothes he instructed his men that they were to pretend to be traveling merchants seeking new places where to trade. Very early in the morning they began their long journey towards the Far North in their dugout Mahogany canoe. For two days they paddled along the coast of the great sea stopping at small islands only to rest at night. Along the way they had encountered other travelers who had been at the Far North city. A good place to trade but be very cautious for these are treacherous people, they had told him. Unfortunately for Chacbe and his men, though, on the morning of the third day which had seem to be a beautiful clear day, after paddling on the open waters for four hours, a huge and terrible storm had come and almost killed him and his three men. It was a severe storm and their canoe had capsized but the men had managed to hung on to it for five hours until they had been washed ashore to a nearby island.

They had lost their weapons and their food and water and had to survive on raw fish for days. On the third day after being stranded on the island they saw a group of men coming towards the island in a huge canoe. Fearing they were people from the North City and since they had no weapons they hid in the nearby mangroves. For two hours they had observed the men who apparently were fishermen who had come to salvage their fish traps after the storm. Chacbe and his three men were surprised when they heard one of the fishermen called to another in their Maya language. "They can't be our people," Chacbe had whispered to his men suspiciously, "we are too far north."

After a while of observing the men and seeing that they actually were wearing clothes typical to the Maya peasants they decided to approach them. They were relieved to hear that they were fishermen belonging to a village from the Chac'temal province but disappointed when they were told that the storm had actually blown them back down South. They were actually not far from the city of Chac'temal, probably three days on foot and two days by canoe. Believing this to be a message from the wind god Chac, Chacbe decided that maybe the gods were not ready for him to go to the City of the Far North yet to execute his revenge. He believed divine intervention had saved them from certain death in the storm. The reason he and his men had been blown back to friendly territories. With that notion in mind and after getting food supplies from the friendly fishermen they headed back to Chac'temal via the sea but not before giving thanks and praises to the gods for miraculously sparing them from death in the storm.

"There will be another time when I can avenge you my father," He whispered to himself. He vowed to one day attempt the journey once more, but until that day came he would continue training to be the best warrior of the Lamanai provinces.

His father was buried, as per tradition, with full military honors, under the earth inside his house. An altar had been erected on the east wall of the house so the family could come and say their prayers. Another house had been built not too far away for Chacbe's mother and the rest of the family by members of his Clan. This is the house where Chacbe grew up; but there wasn't a day growing up when he wouldn't visit his father's tomb and pray at the altar always promising him that when he grew up he would become a warrior and avenge his death. The old Palmetto house that was once beautifully painted, where his father had been interred, was long gone. Destroyed by the forces of nature but the young Chacbe remembered where it was and he still remembered the promise he gave his father in one day avenging him.

Chapter Seven ⁚ ⁚

Box Balam had been playing Pok-A-Tok with his friends as far back as he could remember. They would normally play a game in the afternoon after the boys had finished their school lessons and after doing their chores at home. They had a makeshift ball court in the middle of the Clouds Window Clan's courtyard. The rubber ball was made from the latex resin of the Castilla Tree that grew abundantly in the rainforest. Box's first ball was given to him when he was just a toddler by his uncle Crocodile Tooth and he still had it on a shelf in the corner of his bedroom, it was one of his prized possessions.

He was taught by his father how to recognize a Castilla Tree and how to cut the trunk in a crisscross fashion so that the latex resin of the tree could drain into a waxed cotton bag secured at the bottom of the tree trunk. Later the resin would be boiled in a huge clay pot and before it cooled he would mould the rubber bit by bit until he had a ball about eight inches in diameter. Everybody who tapped a Castilla Tree also knew never to tap it again before one year. A prayer would also be said before taking their sharp flint or obsidian knives to the trees.

In the middle of the Sky Windows Clan's courtyard was a flat circular stone about three feet in diameter where the ball was bounced to begin the game. At one end of the field that was demarcated with sascab, was a post with a hoop ten inches in diameter made with Ti-Tai vine and tied sideways on the post, unlike the Royal Ball Court where the hoop was made from solid rock.

A team usually comprises of eleven members on each team and after the umpire bounced the ball on the middle stone marker the teams try to put the ball through the hoop using only their heads, shoulders, elbows, knees and hips. Professional players always used heavily padded clothing, a helmet and a wooden yoke around their hips. It was very difficult to put the ball through the hoop so normally the first team to do so, won the game; as Chacbe had explained to Box and Red Cat in ceremonial games, where children were not permitted to attend, sometimes one of the losers are usually sacrificed. Then again, sometimes they would only play a friendly game, whereby, the winners won all the jewels that the spectators were wearing. Many times some spectators would run away so they could not be relieved from their jewelry but later they were always caught by the Royal Guards. On opposite sides of the Royal Ball Court were sweat houses for the team. Steam baths for the athletes to be cleansed in body and spirit before the official ceremony preceding the game.

The young boys would usually tie cotton padding on their elbows knees and hips but even so they always ended up with bruises in their bodies after a game. For, even though the ball was made of rubber, it was solid and hard. Box had a team but they were not always available to play. A team for them usually consisted on how many boys were available to play. Many times a one on one or two on two game was played and many times being closely watched by a representative of the Royal Team always on the lookout for new talented players

Even with his bruises Box came out to practice almost every afternoon for he really wanted to be a famous player like his uncle. His uncle, Crocodile Tooth, had always been summoned by Royal Teams of other cities to play with them. He had traveled many times to play in Xunantunich and Caracol and he had even played for the Royal Team of Tikal. He always said that sometimes the game went on for days before a team could score and win. Crocodile Tooth would always come back to Lamanai victorious and with a lot of prizes.

One rainy day when the children were not allowed to practice because it was very dangerous when the ground was wet and slippery, Box went to visit his favorite uncle Crocodile Tooth. Crocodile Tooth only had one son and he had married a girl from Caracol and was now living there, so he lived alone with his wife.

The old chief's son was also a great soldier and ball player. His wife was busy cooking the evening meal when Box got there. "Uncle why are we not allowed to see the Ceremonial Games at the Royal Ball Court," asked Box? Crocodile Tooth had just arrived the day before from patrolling an area beyond Chac'temal and he was very tired but he was also very fond of Box so he answered him by saying, "Like drinking Balche and having a wife is only for grownups, and not for children, so is entering the Royal

Ball Court when a Ceremonial Game is in progress, that is the rule of our ancestors and that is all I am allowed to say to you right now Box." He continued saying, "but I have seen you play ball Box and I am very proud of you. In a few short years you may be selected to play with the royal team. You will then understand a lot of things about our customs and traditions." The veteran warrior and famous ball player looked into Box's eyes and said "Promise me that you will continue practicing hard every time you can."

"I promise uncle," Box had answered.

Box and Red Cat had been by the Ceremonial Ball Court many times when there wasn't a game playing; they had even looked inside the sweat houses where the teams cleansed themselves physically and spiritually before the beginning of a Ceremonial Game. They were fascinated by it and always pictured themselves playing a ceremonial game. Grownups never talked to the children about the outcome of a game even though from far away they could hear them jubilantly shouting cheering and clapping for their team very loudly. Box and all the other children always wondered who were the teams playing and why after the game some people were running away and why sometimes someone was wailing and crying after a game.

Nacom Chacbe had now answered most of the questions from Box Balam and Red Cat, concerning Ceremonial Games that had been in their minds since childhood.

ALTUN—HA
THE HURRICANE
TWENTY YEARS BEFORE

Chapter Eight ···

Altun Ha had not always been the beautiful city it is today and Red Cat knew it well. His father had told him about the fierce storm coming from the Great Waters that had destroyed his beautiful city and killed many people. It had actually taken many years to restore the devastated city of Altun Ha.

Twenty years ago when Red Cat's father was a young man, the fierce hurricane that had destroyed his beloved city had almost killed him. Almost all of the houses surrounding the plazas and all of the valuable crops were destroyed. Altun Ha was so vulnerable to huge storms because of its proximity to the sea.

It was a Tuesday afternoon in the month of October when the high priest announced to the people of Altun Ha that a huge dangerous storm was approaching the coasts of the city. A huge plume of red smoke coming from the very top of one of the highest buildings alerted the people of

Altun Ha of the approaching storm. Even though, the sky had been overcast the past few days, it was rather very calm. The breeze was not blowing and it only rained occasionally. So, when the news of a severe dangerous hurricane was announced, the people were very surprised. The fishermen fishing nearby along the reefs immediately started towards shore and safety. The farmers and field workers also responded to the high priest's call for everyone to seek immediate refuge. Everybody trusted the high priest, he was seldom wrong when predicting the weather.

For many miles around people could see the plume of red smoke. They also knew that it meant a dangerous storm was coming; a blue plume of smoke would mean that the city was under threat of attack by marauders or a foreign army and white smoke meant the city was mourning the death of someone important. Most of the people had fled deep into the jungle with their families, where huge sturdy long log houses had been built amongst huge trees for protection from strong winds, taking only waterproof clothing and food. A lot of people managed to seek refuge in the sturdy built temples and residential areas inside the palaces; but the majority fled into the jungle seeking refuge amongst the huge buttresses of the trees and the log houses.

Unfortunately, Red Cat's father, Silent Cat, was far away in his milpa when he saw the red smoke arising from the city. At the time, he was planting corn using a fire hardened tip, two inches thick stick to make a hole in the ground where he placed a few corn seeds. He was almost finished planting his field with corn when he saw the red smoke coming from the direction of the city, but he decided to stay a while longer and finish up. Before he could finish, though, the breeze started blowing fiercely and it started raining heavily. Everywhere around him he started seeing tree branches swaying and some even breaking off. That was when he realized how serious the situation was. His first thoughts were about his family. He had recently married and his wife was six months pregnant with his first child, so without thinking twice he rushed towards the city four miles away to his clan's plaza, his house and his wife.

His wife was a beautiful girl from Lamanai whom he had met years ago whilst on a trading trip there. Like him, she came from a long line of talented and prosperous farmers. Her father was known for cultivating the best and biggest squash and maniocs of the region.

He did not know it but his wife had already been taken to a safe shelter by the Royal Guards who were in charge of helping anyone who required it in times like these. The fit, hard working young man had only run a couple miles when he tripped on a thick vine growing across the pathway over a steep hill leading to the city. As he came rolling down the hill, all that crossed his mind was his beloved wife and his unborn child. He was also alone in his farm since his brother, who always worked with him at the farm was away on a trading mission in Holpatin. He had gone to sell or trade some of their produce.

When Silent Cat ended at the bottom of hill his head banged against the trunk of a tree and he passed out. When he came to an hour later he was soaking wet and an excruciating pain was on his right leg, he could not move. The wind was howling and small trees were falling everywhere, so no matter how hard he cried for help it was useless. He could barely hear himself; moreover he knew that he had been the last one to leave the milpa of the surrounding area. It was getting dark and he knew that nobody would come looking for him until the hurricane had gone away so he prayed and clung to his faith that he would not die and he would see his wife and one day hold his newborn on his arms.

It wasn't until early the next day when the hurricane had gone subsided that his father and a group of royal guards heard his cries and rescued him. He had endured eleven hours of being wet, unable to move and of severe excruciating pain from a broken ankle.

When the people returned from their shelters deep within the forest, they could not believe what they saw. Most of the city was badly destroyed. All their beautiful houses surrounding their clan's plazas were gone. Not even the eldest person in Altun Ha could remember such devastation before. Nowhere in their history books was such devastation recorded. The only buildings standing were the Royal Palace, the ambassadorial residential area and the Sacred Temples. Many people had been killed by the storm. There were fishermen who didn't make it to shore on time, farmers who decided to stay in their small huts until the skies cleared and many people who were trapped by fallen trees. The trading city of Altun Ha, famous for its Sacred Temple, dedicated to the worship of the Sun God Kinich Ahau had to start anew.

It took a lot of hard work, dedication, and many years but the ruler of Altun Ha and his people managed to restore the city to its past grandiose and beauty. Even though many people moved to cities more inland, being afraid of a similar devastation, Altun Ha prospered and grew even more beautiful.

Silent Cat, after his ordeal during the hurricane, and after his first child was born, decided to move to Lamanai, his wife's native city, and raise his family there, away from the beautiful but very treacherous Great Waters, the sea. It was there that, Red Cat, the athletic and brave companion to Box Balam and Chacbe was born years later.

Chapter Nine ····

Even before the arrow pierced two of the Altun Ha men on the chest, a soldier and a porter taking salt to Lemanai, Chacbe's trained ears had heard the unmistakable whizzing of an arrow in flight. "Take cover" he shouted. But not before two more of his men were also fatally struck with arrows. Other arrows flew dangerously close to their heads and bodies as they flung themselves to the ground. Immediately they formed a ring in a defensive position with weapons in hand. "Anybody sees anything?" Shouted Chacbe but nobody had seen the enemy. "They probably fled," shouted back one of the warriors accompanying them. "They are using the ancient war tactic of attack and run technique and they will probably lay an ambush more ahead." Another of the men shouted back.

Chacbe's party of ten had been walking from Altun Ha towards Lemanai for about five hours now. Five royal guards and two porters from Altun Ha were accompanying them. Now a porter and three soldiers were dead. "We have to change our direction of travel," said Chacbe as he slowly crept to a nearby tree for cover and looking everywhere for the enemy. "We have to walk through the jungle and not on the *sacbeob,*" he said "it is no longer safe, I am sure that now Red Clouds renegades are aware that we know about them slaughtering the merchants and the prince from Altun Ha." They had just gotten on an open area of the jungle that had probably been used for farming and now the farmers had left to fallow when they were ambushed.

"We are the only ones that can take back the message of caution to our city so they are trying to stop us. I am sure that the Serpent Clan Armies are preparing a full scale surprise attack on the allied cities. Listen up men," said Chacbe, "the lives of our people are on our hands, so this is the plan, we will walk through the jungle North towards Holpatin," he said as he pointed on his map that was carefully wrapped in water proof waxed deer skin. "We have no other choice," he added, "They know that we are headed to Lamanai and they will certainly want to spring another ambush up ahead. We have to leave the salt and our food supplies," he said to the men who were very alert, looking everywhere around them trying to see anything suspicious. "Get your weapon ready, getting to Holpatin is our only option if we are to survive," said *Nacom* Chacbe, "we will move silently and we will march in single file, we will all take turns at the end and at the front of the file, make sure," he continued, "that you have your atlatl, bow and arrows and maquahuill always ready. We go North towards Holpatin and Noh Mul there we can request for warriors to accompany us to Lemanai for at this time we know not how many of them may be preparing to attack us again and with the tactics they are using it's almost impossible to defeat them."

After burying their dead Chacbe and his men headed North through the jungle, it had started raining and they could hear the monkeys howling overhead having been disturbed by the humans going through their territory. It was very hot and even though the rain was falling, the mosquitoes were still biting them and following them every step of the way. Later that evening the rain had stopped but darkness was approaching and the men were wet, very tired and hungry for they had to abandon most of their food supplies, they were only eating nuts and berries that they found along the way. There was no way they were going to light a fire, not if they wanted to give away their position.

Late in the evening as they were wading across a shallow creek, Red Cat pointed to a cluster of ripe and juicy looking *Hawactes*. Breaking ranks he waded towards the far side of the bank of the creek where he had seen the ripe cluster of *Hawactes* on the tree that was full of sharp thorns. Just as he was about to cut a bunch of the fruit; Box Balam and the rest of the group heard him cry in pain. As they rushed to him to see what was the matter they noticed a huge Yellow Jawed Snake chopped in three pieces. The snake had been killed by Red Cat but not before sinking its fangs in his left ankle five times.

Red Cat laid about three feet from the snake and the men could clearly see how his foot was already beginning to swell and turn red. "Quick," said one of the soldiers get a piece of Ti-Tai vine and tie his leg and I will try to suck the poison out." This was indeed a desperate move to save the boy but everybody knew, even Red Cat himself, that that nobody had ever survived the bite of the demonic and feared Fer-De-Lance snake. As much as the men tried, by tying his leg to stop the flow of the poison and cutting where the punctured wounds of the fangs of the snake was and sucking on it to extract the poison by spitting it out Red Cat was dead in less than two hours. Tears came to Box Balams eyes as he remembered that only, hours ago, as they guarded their camp while the other men rested, they whispered silently about playing Pok-A-Tok in the Ceremonial Ball Court of Lemanai. Box Balam had explained to him what Chacbe had told him about the Ceremonial Games that children were not allowed to witness, when he was visiting his family at Altun Ha.

"It's because," he told him, "the Royal Team many times played with captive enemies of Lemanai and after the game," he said, "one of the captive enemies team was always sacrificed, his heart was ceremoniously cut out and then offered to Lord Kinich Ahau or even Chac. The rest of the captive enemies were always kept locked up until another Ceremonial Game was played."

He had told Red Cat that the Royal Team of Lemanai after winning, were always given a feast in their honor and they were also given many precious gifts; But if they lost the game then all the members of the Royal Team were disposed of all their jewelry and were ordered to fast inside the sweat house for two days. Red Cat had whispered to Box "We will always be winners Box Balam," Red Cat had answered. "Yes." Box had then said," and we will be rich and I will marry Ixchell Quetzal."

As Red Cat was being buried, with tears in his eyes Box Balam said to him; "Go on my friend, where you go you will play Pok- A-Tok with the Hero Twins and just as they tricked the lords of Xibalba and defeated them so shall you come out victorious from the underworld and into heaven with your ancestors.

The legend of the Hero Twins was known throughout the Maya Empires it was recorded in the Sacred Book the

Popol Vuh hundreds of years ago. It was believed that all the Maya People were descendants of the Hero twins Hunapuh and Xbalanque the Sun and the Moon. A beautiful sacred story of light conquering darkness and life prevailing over death. "Go in peace Red Cat, my friend, for your ancestors are waiting for you," whispered Box Balam.

The next day as the men pressed northward towards Holpatin they could hear the unmistakable croaking sound of the Keel Billed Toucan bird encouraging them to keep on going. The noisy *Chachalacas* could also be heard in the distance. It was very hot and humid, the men were tired and hungry and the

Mosquitoes were feeding on frenzy. In spite of all this, the men kept on pushing towards Holpatin.

Unknown to Chacbe and his men, in Lamanai, a huge army had been mustered and was getting ready to march towards Noh Mul where they would be united with the small but very efficient army of Altun Ha and Holpatin to defend Chac'temal from the invading armies of the Serpent Clan, presumably under the command of Red Cloud and his son Nohoch Pek. The brother of Box Balam, Big Tapir, had been appointed commander of the allied forces by the war council of the allied cities. He was also to be under the advice of retired army chiefs like Crocodile Tooth and others.

A deep trench was being dug on the North and West sides of the city of Lamanai and able guards had strategically been placed on all corners of the city as lookouts. Not that the army chiefs and captains ever believed that the foreign army would infiltrate so far inland, but they wanted to be on the safe side. The lagoon formed a natural defense for the city on the East and the South sides but still a huge wall and platform for soldiers to stand, on was being built on the banks of the lagoon by every able bodied men of Lamanai.

A section of soldiers of Altun Ha patrolling the area had encountered the shallow grave of the four men killed the day before. The grave had been partially dug up by scavenging animals and the soldiers had recognized the four bodies as royal soldiers and a porter from their city. They identified the arrows that killed them as foreign made and immediately reported their find to their chief and ruler. Immediately a contingent of royal soldiers from Altun Ha was dispatched to Lamanai, Holpatin, Noh Mul and Chac'temal to inform their rulers about the incident and to start preparing for possible war.

Once more the Sacred Conch Shell inlaid with Mother of Pearl and shiny Green Jade, atop the tallest temple in Lamanai had been blown on the four directions of the cardinal points. This time, not calling the people of Lamanai for celebration but to prepare for a dreadful war.

Chapter Ten ═══

Two days after the army had departed Lamanai towards Chac'temal and no word had been sent back about Chacbe, Box and Red Cat. The people and families of Chacbe and his men started mourning for them, fearing them dead. Ixchel Quetzal and Box's younger sister Ek Balam held hands tightly with tears in their eyes as they walked towards the shrine dedicated to the supreme god Hunab Ku located at the Far East corner of the Clouds Window's Clan Plaza.

School for them had been closed in order to give the people time to prepare for war and to mourn their loved ones. As they laid a polychrome vase of burning copal and a bouquet of aromatic flowers at the base of the shrine the two young maidens fell on their knees and began praying for the souls of the dead and safe return of the three missing men, Chacbe, Box Balam, and Red Cat.

Both Ixchel Quetzal and Ek Balam were wearing the same long white cotton dress with red flowers embroidered on the hems and sleeves and the sky blue shawl they had worn at the Luum Mak ceremonies just a few days ago. Ixchel had found out that Box was Ek's brother and had confided in her that she had fallen in love with Box on the day of the *Luum Mak*. Specially, she had said to her that he was very brave by asking her name when she had brought the *Balche* drink to him. "Imagine," she had said, "if one of the Chilams had heard him talking during the ceremony he would have surely been punished." She was actually counting the hours when he would be back from his mission and could see him again. She looked towards the heaven from her kneeling position and still crying, prayed even harder for his safe return.

"Have faith Ixchel," Ek said gently with hope in her heart, "he is alive and he is probably hiding somewhere safe, waiting for the appropriate time to return home."

"My uncle who is also a holy man and one of the Chilams has told me the same thing," answered Ixchel. "He also told me that that the *Nacom* Chacbe and Box had appeared to him in a vision while he was fasting and praying. He believes they are still alive somewhere. Since he didn't see Red Cat in his vision he believes he might be dead." Ek looked at Ixchel and said, "I really hope that your uncle is wrong about Red Cat. I have known him since we were very little and I was always very fond of him. He was very athletic and he always played ball with Box."

A huge black cloud had covered the sun and a strong breeze started blowing. "We must go to the palace now," said Ek, "it looks like a big storm is coming." They ran towards the palace holding up their long white dresses, their long black braided hair flapping in the wind.

Every girl of Ixchel and Ek's age were expected at the palace that morning. The elders and high priest would be assigning them different jobs to help in the war effort. Some of the girls would be aides to the medicine women, some would be repairing and sewing new armors made from tapir hides for the soldiers at war. Some of the women would be preparing food that would be taken to Chac'temal for the fighting soldiers. Lord Nohoch Zak Mai, the Ruler, his wife and the princess Shining Blue Star as well as the High Priest and his Acolytes were to stay inside their palace guarded by a section of the Jaguar Order Warriors during the war.

For Ixchel and Ek, though, the High Priest had a special job. They were to accompany him and his Chilams to a cave south of the city which they believed was one of the entrances to the underworld. Deities and the spirits of some of their ancestors were believed to be passing through there. They would be escorted by five Royal Guards to the caves and back. The High Priest and his Chilams would enter the cave and after fasting and praying for two days, would perform a special ceremony and sacrifice thirteen Keel Billed Toucans one for each of the layers of heaven and its gods leading to heaven. They would be praying for the safe return of the sons of Lamanai at war. The girls' job was to make sure that the incensories placed on each side of the cave entrance was always filled with Copal and that it stayed lit for all the time the Holy Men would be inside the cave, also known as Xibalba, portals to the underworld.

When Chief Big Tapir heard about the death of the Altun Ha men accompanying Chacbe and fearing that they were Nohoch Pek's men who had also killed the young Altun Ha prince Zac Chen, decided to appoint two personal guards for his aging uncle Crocodile Tooth. He rightly suspected that since Red Cloud son was in the area he might be looking for revenge for his father and may try to kill the retired army chief Crocodile Tooth. Big Tapir knew all about Red Clouds treason in Chac'temal and his hatred for the retired chief for foiling his attempt in becoming ruler of the Chac'temal provinces and forcing him into exile. Even retired, Crocodile Tooth was still considered by the army chief of Lamanai and other cities, as one of the most brilliant army chiefs in history. He was considered very important and they needed him for consultations in regards to war and defense tactics.

NOHOCH PEK
AND HIS BAND OF
RENEGADES

CHAPTER ELEVEN

Since the day that Nohoch Pek had embarked on the secret mission for his father Red Cloud, he had had no real rest. He was determined to bring back Chief Crocodile Tooth's Jade pendant he wore around his neck, back to his father, after killing him. The pendant presented to him by the ruler of Chac'temal declaring him a hero and honorary citizen of Chac'temal for his help in driving back the invading army of the Far North.

After going by canoes via the great waters, bypassing Chac'temal and Holpatin, he and his men, after hiding their canoes, marched through the jungle between Altun Ha and Holpatin. From there they would steal canoes then head South on the Dzuluinicob River to the outskirts of Lamanai.

After getting there for three days he and his men had laid in the surrounding jungle waiting for the opportunity to kill the old warrior, but every time there was something preventing him from doing so. His orders were clear, he was to raise no suspicion as to who had killed him, it must look like the work of common thieves; but there were always four or five people in Crocodile Tooth's house. Mostly young soldiers that would come to seek advice in the use of foreign weapons captured from foreigners that had come to steal in the area. At night, Royal Guards always patrolled the perimeters of the city, so killing Crocodile Tooth became almost impossible for Nohoch Pek.

The reason was that they should not be recognized, His father was specific about that, he was afraid that he or one of his men could be killed or injured in his attempt to kill the retired warrior and their identity revealed. That would definitely foil any attempt in trying to invade Chac'temal

He was hiding in the bushes by the Clouds Window's Clan courtyard before and during the Luum Mak Ceremony studying the every move of Crocodile Tooth. One of the older warriors, Nicte, knew him well so he had pointed him out to Nohoch Pek. Nicte had also been one of Red Clouds personal royal guards that had attempted to execute Crocodile Tooth and his captains and had left Crocodile Tooth almost dead. He had escaped into the jungle when word was out that all of Red Clouds personal guards were being arrested. He had later joined Red Cat and his family on his way to the Far North city.

Nohoch Pek was becoming very desperate and very nervous. They had committed a very serious mistake, days ago, and, he suspected that warriors from Altun Ha would be seeking the robbers that had killed the young prince and the merchants. He had had no idea that one of the merchants had survived.

After ambushing the group of merchants in their canoes in the river, they hoped only to take away their goods, and treasures, a little reward for his men to take back home; But everything had gone terribly wrong. After a merchant had told one of his men that he knew him and that he, Nohoch Pek, looked like the son of Red Cloud. They decided there and then that they should kill all of them; even after the chief merchant declared that they could take everything but should spare their lives in order for them to take the prince of Altun Ha back home safely; But Nohoch Pek wasn't about to take the chance to foil his father's attempt in invading Chac'temal so he ordered all of them be killed. They had to protect their identities. He was worried though, if it had been only merchants they had robbed and killed, they would probably had attributed it to robbers who usually came from the highlands and they would have only advised other merchants to be extra careful next time they traveled. They probably wouldn't have gone to extremes in pursuing the robbers.

With the death of a prince it was different Nohoch Pek knew, they would send their soldiers in full force to find the ones responsible for the death of the young prince. He had hurried on to Lamanai as fast as he could, but always hiding in the jungle and being very careful not to be seen, to try to accomplish his mission. It had been three days now and he was getting extremely restless, moreover now he had heard some farmers talking about an injured merchant in Holpatin claiming that it was the son of Red Cloud that had ordered the execution of the young prince Zac Chen and his colleagues. He knew that when the ruler of the Northern City Lord *Tepocoatle* and his High Priest found out that he was involved in the slaying of the prince of Altun Ha, they would be very mad and his father would be in great danger. His father had specifically told him that this was to be a very secret mission. Lord *Tepocoatl* should never know for he had ordered Red Cloud to stay away from Chac'temal and its allied cities until after he decided if he was to help him invade Chac'temal.

Now the ruler of the Cloud Serpent Clan would be furious for they would not be able to mount a surprise attack on the allied cities if they had decided to do so. Nohoch Pek dreaded to go back home empty handed and face the wrath of his father and the ruler. He had to go back though, and explain what had happened. As a last resort and desperate move he decided to kill the three men heading for Altun Ha. He had heard that one of the boys was Crocodile Tooth's nephew and by taking his necklace back to his father his punishment wouldn't be so severe. He decided to wait to when they were returning back so he could capture one of them alive and find out what were the plans of the ruler of Altun Ha in regards to who had killed his son.

The ambush they had sprung on Chacbe, Box, and the rest of the group had failed miserably. They didn't expect them to be escorted back by soldiers of Altun Ha, there were too many of them and they had only managed to kill four of them. The rest of the group had taken another direction through the jungle going north. This made Nohoch Pek very mad for he had expected to kill them all swiftly, head to where their canoes were hidden, then paddle home to safety. He had the look of a mad man when he said to his six men, "We will find and kill them all if it's the last thing we do here on earth. They will never get to Lamanai or any other city alive." Nicte and his fanatic warriors who had sworn to protect him until death, only shook their head, readied their weapons, and followed their determined leader.

THE SACRED JAGUAR

Chapter Twelve

Even though the rain forest abounded with food, the female Jaguar was very hungry. She had not eaten for forty-two hours. She had been hunting since then but without luck. She had even dared to go beyond her territory but all to no avail. Now, she had come across the fresh tracks and scent of an Agouti and she was determined to catch it. She walked silently towards where she could hear it feeding under a huge Mamee tree. She was an expert hunter so she walked on the opposite side so that the wind wouldn't carry her scent towards the Agouti. This was her last chance since she was getting tired and weak, she was heavy with pregnancy and this slowed her movements drastically.

The mother to be, now, had to rely on her cunning and hunting experience, and not her physical agility this time to hunt successfully. So, when the wind shifted she also shifted trying to hide her scent. Crouching, she moved noiselessly and slowly towards her prey. It was the biggest and fattest

Agouti she had seen for months and she could almost taste its blood in her mouth. When she had gotten close enough, with one big leap she jumped at her food; but the Agouti had seen her at the last minute and she also leaped aside.

If it wasn't for a huge vine that was hanging from the tree, it would have eluded the powerful paws of the hungry female Jaguar. On a last desperate move to escape the predator the Agouti had jumped straight unto the big fat vine. With one big slap with her powerful left paw, the hungry Jaguar had secured her food. Her mighty claws had dug deep into the belly of the frightened prey disemboweling her and killing it almost instantly. She then dragged her food about fifty feet to a nearby tree, climbed to a thick limb and savored her food This was enough food to keep her satisfied for a few days. Now, it was time to find a nice cozy spot where she could give birth safely to her babies. She knew the exact spot; she had spotted a small cave hidden by thick bushes just a few days ago. So, after finishing her meal and drinking her fill of water, at the Dzuluinicob River nearby, she headed slowly but satisfied towards her den to be.

Just a few days ago, though, she had heard the shouting and war cries of the humans doing battle. At the beginning her instincts and past experience with humans screamed to her to stay away, far, far away. She knew that in the scheme of things, the wise thing to do was to put great distances between her and the treacherous humans who didn't kill Jaguars because they were hungry but because they wanted to wear her beautiful yellow and black coat as clothes.

She attempted to do just that, but she was terribly hungry and it got the best of her. She was getting weak and being so heavy with pregnancy she could not move fast enough. Moreover, humans were meat and she desperately needed to eat meat. The scrawny Iguana she had eaten earlier had only made her even hungrier. Silently and cautiously she climbed a huge tree and hid between its branches.

She was extremely afraid of humans; as a matter of fact she hated them too. As a juvenile she had narrowly escaped the sharp end of their spears but her sibling and mother hadn't been so lucky. She still carried a big scar on her back where the spear had cut her. A few inches lower and she would have suffered the same fate as her family. For generations they had been hunted and killed by humans so staying away from humans was embedded in her instincts. She knew that the humans respected them. Why then did they kneel in front of her dead mother and sibling looking up in the sky while chanting and swinging a smoking container over their bodies? That same instinct that urged her to stay far away from humans was the same instinct that told her that the dreaded humans were wicked and malicious. It was quite clear that they held them in great esteem yet they still killed them. Not because they were hungry but because they wanted to wear their skins as coats.

The Jaguars were not the largest animal of the rainforest, the Tapir was; but they were the fastest and most powerful, so they were the Kings and Queens of the Rain forest.

She stood silently observing the humans kill one another. The mother to be had actually seen when Chacbe was struck from behind with a spear impaling and killing him instantly. She had also seen when Box Balam had struck Chacbe's killer with an arrow in the throat also killing him. She observed as Box checked his companions for signs of life then looking very confused and hurt fled into the jungle.

She had been patient before, she had actually lay-waited a prey for days waiting for the right time to kill it. At that particular time she had killed a huge Red Brocket deer. With one swift move she had jumped at it striking it like a missile. At that time though, her body was in splendid condition. She was lean and had tight muscles. She would also wait today, she was hungry but there could be more humans around so she waited and waited . . . .

The female Jaguar had waited for over two hours when she finally decided to inspect the carnage about fifty feet from her hideout. She had just descended the safety of the tree when she heard human voices. She immediately hid between the thick brushes around the buttress of the tree. They were soldiers from Altun Ha and after checking the dead people they began shouting for Box Balam. Upon hearing the vocal commotion of the humans the frightened animal then fled into the jungle. She remembered the injured boy fleeing into the jungle and picking up his scent decided to go after him.

For days she stalked the injured boy, surviving only on small lizards and rodents she killed along the way. The boy was injured and looked weak so she was waiting for the appropriate time for her to attack him. More than once she had decided to attack her prey when night was falling, but every time he would find the strength to start a fire. The female Jaguar dreaded the humans but she extremely dreaded fire even more. Fire and humans were a deadly combination for her.

The injured Box Balam didn't have the faintest idea how close he was in being eaten by one of the Lords of the Rain Forest. His mind was only set in finding a village or a milpa so he could get help. At night when he rested he had no idea that the fires he lit had actually saved his life. So it was then, that the night before he was rescued, the pregnant Jaguar had come across two live White Lipped Peccaries hanging from their feet, head down from a small tree. They were the snare-traps of a Maya hunter. After killing the peccaries she feasted on one of them and dragged the other one on the highest branch of a far away tree for later consumption. She was then no longer interested in the human prey. A week later and the day after she had hunted and eaten the fat Agouti, she gave birth to two robust baby Jaguars.

The gods had spared the young aspiring soldier and ball player from being food for the Sacred Jaguar. Box Balam would probably never know this, not in this life . . . .

Chapter Thirteen

After many days of wandering alone in the forest almost starving and delirious with high fever caused by an infection, Box Balam, came across a small milpa being tended by a farmer and his son. He approached them because he knew that he had to be somewhere between the cities of Holpatin and Noh Mul and they had to be people friendly to his city. When the farmers saw him they immediately dropped their planting stick and grabbed their war clubs. They were farmers from Holpatin and they had been cautioned about robbers being in the area and they were going to defend their precious cacao and corn seeds with their lives if necessary.

This was unnecessary since Box fell to the ground groaning even before he could identify himself. The farmers upon seeing that the young man coming from the jungle was obviously seriously injured and probably dying rushed to his aid. "My name is Box Balam," Box weakly whispered, "I am the son of the Cloud Window's Clan, of the city of Lamanai subject to Lord Nohoch Zak Mai of the Great Jaguar Clan, Ruler of the Lamanai Territories and Dzuluinicob." Is all he could barely whisper to the farmer and his son.

"It's ok my son," the old farmer said to him, "Say no more please, you must save your energy for you are injured and very sick. We know who you are and your people in Lamanai will be happy to know that you are alive," he said while putting a calabash gourd with fresh water to Box's lips. "Soldiers have been looking for you all over. You are safe now and we will take care of you. The people who did this to you are all dead." That was the last thing Box heard before he succumbed to his injuries and pain. A peaceful feeling overcame his entire body and spirit as he drifted into darkness.

In his dream, Box could feel the cold touch of a huge Yellow Jawed snake wrapped around his neck, the snake facing, him threatening to sink his long yellow venomous fangs in his face. Red Cat was nearby dead with a hundred snakes crawling on top of him including the very beautiful but equally venomous red black and yellow Coral snakes. Their colors were so bright and beautiful that if it was made from wood it could fit perfectly as a bracelet on a maiden's wrist.

"No, no, no!" He could hear himself screaming as he woke up and saw a kind looking old lady putting a bowl of a very bitter liquid to his mouth, urging him to drink. He was sweating profusely and his body was shaking uncontrollably. The kind old medicine woman put a damp cloth on his forehead at the same time saying, "It's ok now my son, it was only a bad dream, your life is out of danger now. Drink this, it will help you heal." Box Balam looked at the gentle short old lady wondering if he was somewhere in the underworld trying to make his way into heaven. "relax son," the old lady repeated to him, "you are clean now, all the leaches and Botfly larvae have been expelled from your body and the arrow wounds in your side and arm are now healing very well, praise our Goddess Ixchell," she added, "one more day in the jungle and you would have never made it. So it was good you came across the milpa and the farmers when you did."

Box Balam looked at the old woman with his heart filled with gratitude and every time he tried to open his mouth to say something, she would silent him with a shshsh and say, "don't speak just relax and try to sleep some more." After the old medicine woman left the room another woman entered with a bowl of fresh water and began cleaning his wound before adding a paste medicine on it. He could still feel the bitter taste in his mouth of the medicine the old lady had given him and he welcomed it knowing that a bitter medicine was always a good medicine. *Once more, he fell on a deep but restless sleep filled with nightmares of snakes, leeches, Botfly larvae and people trying to kill him.*

Before the badly injured Box had come across the farmer and his son, his companions had all been killed in an ambush. Box, Chacbe, and his men had been wading across a swamp trying to be silent and the same time moving their spears around in the dark murky waters of the swamp trying to frighten away any crocodile that may be brave enough to come near them. Just as they had stepped on dry land, they were once more attacked by Nohoch Pek and his men. For two days Nohoch Pek had been following Chacbe and his men looking for the right time to attack.

Box had seen three of his colleagues fall back into the swamp with arrows sticking from their chest. Chacbe had seen the enemy hiding in the nearby bushes and with club in hands he ran towards them attacking them savagely, shouting the cries of war. He saw blood spilling as one, and then another of the enemies fell to the ground. Chacbe was attacking like a crazed Jaguar and another one had fallen with his face smashed and bleeding profusely. Box Balam had taken careful aim and had struck one of the enemies with his arrow.

As he grabbed his *Maquahuill*, and ran towards the enemy, he was struck with a studded club on his side. That didn't stop him, he continued running towards his enemy and struck one of them in the face with his club, blood spraying all over him. He could see Chacbe wrestling with the one who appeared to be the leader, at the same time slinging another arrow. Chacbe had sunk his sharp flint knife in the chest of Nohoch Pek but being blinded by blood and a wound in his face he could not see one of the enemy that was hiding behind the trunk of a tree coming from behind with a spear. Before Box could shout a warning Chacbe was impaled with the spear. At the same time Box released his arrow striking Nicte, the last of the enemy, on the left side of his chest. It was a battle that had caused him his life but Chacbe had finally avenged his father by killing some of the very people that many years ago had murdered his father at Chac'temal.

Feeling very confused seeing his mentor and all of his colleagues dead and with a club wound on his side Box looked desperately for the signs of more enemies. He couldn't see anybody else so, he quickly checked his friends for signs of life but all of them were dead including Nacom Chacbe. Fearing that there may be more enemies nearby, still clutching his war club, made a dash for cover and refuge into the thick and inhospitable jungle. He had been wondering through the very thick and desolate jungle surviving only on Cohune Nuts, wild Papayas, *Hawactes* and water from the Water Vine for five days until he came across the *milpa* or small farm, the kind farmer and his son.

CITY OF THE FAR NORTH

THE CLOUD SERPENT CLAN

Chapter Fourteen

"You disobeyed me and by doing so you have offended the honor of The Clouds Serpent Clan and the people of The Northern Cities," Lord *Tepocoatle* (Tepokwatle) shouted loudly at Red Cloud pointing his finger in his face. The High Priest and War Chief were standing behind the ruler also looking down at Red Cloud looking very mad. Red Cloud had been arrested the day before and now he lay on his knees, with his hands tied behind his back in front of the ruler and the council of the Far North City. He was being accused for treason and for disobeying direct orders given by the ruler. He had been beaten and humiliated in front of hundreds of people in the plaza below now he was facing the wrath of the council members.

"You were given specific orders not to send your men on any more espionage missions until our High Priests, war chiefs and elders had consulted with our gods and ancestors," Lord *Tepocoatle* continued, "You betrayed us by sending your son and his guard to wreak havoc in the Allied Cities. They committed a serious and stupid mistake by killing the prince of Altun Ha and worse of all, by leaving one of his men alive that had recognized him and his guard, Nicte. My sources tell me that they now believe that we were the ones who had sent them on an espionage mission. This has prompted the Allied Cities to go on a state of war preparedness and defense."

The High Priest pointed his ceremonial staff angrily at Red Cloud and said, "because of the death of the young prince, even Las Milpas, Caracol, and Xunantunich have joined forces in alliance with Lamanai and Altun Ha to help defend Chac'temal and Cerros. Our sources tell us that there are at least six thousand warriors stationed in the Chac'temal provinces."

"Our patrols cannot venture beyond our border without fear of being attacked," added the War Chief of the Northern City. As you may probably know we were almost ready for a full scale invasion to Chac'temal, without raising the suspicion of the Allied Cities. We had planned a different strategy this time and we were going to attack from the West side and not from the Great Waters this time." He lifted Red Cloud's face with his sharp pointed spear and angrily added, "what you wanted to do was a stupid act of revenge, and yes, we know about it, and now your son Nohoch Pek and his guards are all dead and Crocodile Tooth is still alive, our chances of invading the wealthy city of Chac'temal is gone all because of your stupid revenge. Our chance of a military campaign against Chac'temal is over, you foolish, foolish man." The War Chief shouted at Red Cloud. "All the other rulers and high priests of the other Northern Cities are holding us responsible for foiling our opportunity in invading Chac'temal and Cerros" he gruffly said.

Lord *Tepocoatle* who had calmed himself and had sat down on his throne with hand rests resembling serpents with their jaws open and ominous yellow fangs showing, lifted his right arm signaling everyone to be quiet. All of this time Red Cloud had been on his knees, his hands tied behind him with his body full of bruises feeling very miserable. He was silently crying but not because of what would become of him, for at this point he really didn't care, but because he felt responsible for the death of his beloved son and not knowing what would be the fate of the rest of his family.

Lord *Tepocoatle* touched Red Cloud's head with his scepter and slowly said, "We were happy to give refuge, sanctuary and protection to you, your family and followers when you were expelled from your city. All these years you have worked hard and have brought riches from your raids to other cities, to ours and for that we were always thankful. We also appreciated that you had chosen our city for refuge. You brought to us a wealth of knowledge and information about the defenses of our enemies of the South." Red Cloud without saying a word pleadingly looked not on the face of *Tepocoatle* but beyond him. The ruler continued saying, "by disobeying our orders and by sending your son to Lamanai without our consent, you have committed one of the most grievous and unholy act to The Cloud Serpent Clan, the High Priests and all the people of the Northern Cities."

"In order to appease our angry gods especially *Quetzalcoatle* the Serpent God, you and two of your personal guards will be sacrificed at dawn tomorrow. This is the only way we will be at peace with him and our ancestors in not being able to invade Chac'temal. As from now you will be fed the best food, and dressed in your ceremonial attire. You will be readied to go to *Quetzalcoatle*," added the High Priest.

The Ruler of The Northern City had always liked Red Cloud but there was nothing he could do to save his life. The High Priest had informed him that, *Quetzalcoatle* had appeared to him in a vision and that he was very angry with the people of the Cloud Serpent Clan for not being able to invade their enemies and that he demanded human blood.

The ruler touched Red Cloud in his head and said, "Because you have served us loyally in the past years your family and the family's of your people who followed you here will be declared citizens of our city they will be allowed to form their own clan and make their own courtyard. They will also have to forget about Chac'temal and it shall never be mentioned to their children and their children after that," he said. "It will be unlawful for any of your surviving family and followers to mention the name of the land of their birth and anyone disobeying will be punished with death." He concluded at the same time reaching for a golden cup filled with a yellowish looking wine.

That made Red Cloud even sadder knowing that his grandchildren and descendants may never know that they had come from a noble Royal Lineage that could be traced back hundreds of years. Even though he knew that a terrible death awaited him, he felt sad but content knowing that his family had been spared and will have a place to call home. "Maybe one day one of my descendants will find out about our efforts in trying to recover our rightful place in the palaces of Chac'temal," thought Red Cloud with a last hope in his heart. "Then he will carry out my revenge and become King and Ruler of the land of his ancestors Chac'temal."

The day before he was arrested, he had rightfully suspected that the mission to Lamanai had been a complete failure. Deep in his heart he knew that his son and all of his guards were dead. He had seen when foreign merchants had gone to see the High Priest with messages and information about the cities where they traded. He had seen the merchants from the south looking at him suspiciously. There was also talk around the plazas that a young prince had been murdered near Holpatin and that Chact'temal and the Sister Cities were preparing for war.

He knew that it would not be long before he got arrested and he had resigned himself. He could not deny his participation in the mission it could only create more danger to the rest of his family, his wife, his two adolescent daughters and his seven year old son. Even the families of his loyal followers would be in deadly danger if he denied his participation. Moreover the Ruler and High Priest knew that his son or any of his guards, for that matter, would never go on a mission without his permission.

So, when from his window he saw Royal Guards approaching his house he immediately instructed his crying wife and children that they were to say nothing and deny any knowledge of his son Nohoch Pek's whereabouts. "We cannot escape," he had told her when she had mentioned it. "We would surely be found then all of us could be executed. I alone must accept responsibility and you all must be strong." He looked deep into the eyes of his wife and three children and said, "I am sure that you will be denied the mentioning of our beloved Chac'temal to one another for that is the custom here but you must never forget that you are royalty, son and daughters of a King and Queen. Please, always mention it to your children and them to their children after that but every time in secrecy. You have to be very careful that no one hears you for you will be in grave danger."

Five minutes after that he was yanked from the arms of his wailing loved ones. He was then tied and dragged to the center of the Royal Plaza where he was flogged by a Royal Guard then ridiculed and humiliated by hundreds of onlookers.

Lord Tepocoatle's long headdress of beautiful bright colored feathers rustled in the wind as he hurriedly left the Royal Courtroom towards his palace. He was wearing turtle shaped ear flares made of pure gold. Around his wrists and ankles were golden bracelets and anklets in shapes of serpents with their mouths open and fangs showing. He had on a tunic of the finest textile and the skin of a Puma with its head still attached was wrapped around his right shoulder. Tattoos of snakes and other animals covered parts of his body. The golden thick chains and pendants on his tunic glittered in the sunlight.

Unlike the Maya People of the Southern Cities who preferred the shiny green Jade as their treasure and jewelry, the people of the Northern Cities preferred gold.

As soon as the Ruler and the high Priest disappeared into the palace, the War Chief ordered two of his guards to seize Red Cloud and ordered that he be taken to the Sacred Temple of *Quetzalcoatle*. Once there, very quiet and without putting any resistance, his body was cleansed, and it was completely covered in a vivid blue paint made from a mixture of indigo dye and a type of clay. Pieces of paper had also been threaded through both of his earlobes just as it was done in Chac'temal and as he had seen it done many, many times before, to sacrificial victims here in the Northern City. At the crack of dawn the next day, his heart still beating, was ripped from his chest and offered to the god *Quetzalcoatle*.

THE CAVES

"XIBALBA"

CHAPTER FIFTEEN

As the High Priest of Lamanai, SacPek, emerged from the caves, where they had been performing rituals and offerings to their ancestors and gods for the past three days, the Royal Guards guarding the cave entrance and the two girls Ek and Ixchel who were holding the Copal censer fell to their knees. The girls began swinging the incense burner back and forth chanting and giving praises that the High Priest and *Chilams* had returned from the underworld victorious.

For three days the High Priest and his assistance had eaten nothing but Hallucinogenic Mushrooms and drinking Holy Water dripping from the stalactites of the cave, performing rituals invoking the gods and their ancestors in an altered state of consciousness. Every day they had sacrificed some of the Keel Billed Toucans they had taken with them. Every time they prayed they implored the gods for a vision in how to win the war at Chac'temal. On the last day, they ate the hearts of the last birds and this time praying for peace and that the foreign armies change their minds from wanting war against the Allied Cities. As they were stepping down from the mouth of the cave two huge lovely iridescent Blue Morpho butterflies flew past in front of them. As hungry and tired as they were the old High Priest and his Chilams smiled broadly upon seeing the beautiful butterflies, knowing and understanding the meaning of their presence.

On the last day inside the cave, in a vision, the High Priest had seen the heart of Red Cloud being ripped off his chest by the High Priest of the Northern City. In another vision he had seen a city completely painted in red and he also saw warriors entering the city defeated and with their heads bowed in shame. In his vision he recognized the city as one of the Northern Cities with their defeated army.

The High Priest of Lamanai, Lord Sac Pek, had correctly translated these clear visions as Red Cloud being dead and that the ruler of the Northern Cities had heard about the great allied armies camped around Chac'temal and Cerros. Fearing on being defeated and having more casualties than the last time, had surrendered the idea, and opted not to declare war against Chac'temal anymore.

So after emerging from the caves and upon seeing the Iridescent Blue Morpho Butterflies fly past them, was all they needed to confirm that the translation of the visions was exactly as the High Priest had translated it. The presence of two Blue Morpho butterflies floating in the wind in front of them was exactly what they needed to see, in order to put their ruler and the people of Lamanai and its sister cities at peace.

Chapter Sixteen

Ambassadors of the friendly cities residing in Lamanai had been waiting patiently for the return of the Holy Men to enlighten them on what next step should be taken by their cities in regards to the war. Many cities could not afford a war right now. The city of Copan, for example, for two years now was having a lot of trouble keeping its people fed. Hurricanes for two consecutive years had devastated the villages and farms of Copan and their raised fields had been completely washed away.

Only a third of their vegetables planted had been reaped and their warehouses were running very short in food supplies. The people of Copan had been rationing their food and the less fortunate people were actually barely surviving from the flour made from the nuts of the Breadnut trees. Also known as the *Ramon* tree, it was a nut producing tree that required no specialized cultivation; but which's nuts provided a good source of protein. For that reason many of the Copan citizens were beginning to migrate north to other more prosperous Maya cities, far away from Copan.

For the rulers of Copan, this was not good, since, by losing the peasants, they not only lost very good farmers but they also lost the young men that could one day become skilled masons. They needed the farmers but they also desperately needed their sons to help them build their temples and palaces.

Moreover, there was a lot of talk between the peasants and farmers of Copan that the ruler and High Priests of their cities were greedy and selfish and they only cared about their families and the ones close to them. The gods, they believe were punishing the city of Copan because of the selfish, lavish lifestyle of their Royal Families and the fortunate few. Word was also out that one of the elite clans of Copan was plotting to overthrow the present ruler. Preparing for war only made it worse for the future of the Maya city of Copan.

This was the reason that the ruler of Copan had sent an emissary to hear the High Priest's message and join his ambassador in Lamanai to try to convince Lord Nohoch Zak Mai to loan him food and seeds for his hungry people. In payment the Ruler of Copan would then pledge two hundred men to work in the plantations or orchards of the prosperous city of Lamanai for an undetermined amount of time. His soldiers and farmers were already rebuilding the raised fields and terraced hills used for planting but they were in desperate need of new seeds to replant it.

"Citizens of Lamanai and visiting dignitaries of our sister cities," The great orator and High Priest of Lamanai, Lord Sac Pek, was saying loudly, addressing the people who had gathered in a multitude in the Ceremonial Plaza in front of The Sacred Temple. He and his Chilams were standing on the lower balcony of the temple they had been cleansed, well fed and they were dressed in their full ceremonial regalia. On the balcony of the Royal Palace stood Lord Nohoch Zak Mai, his family and Crocodile Tooth the retired War Chief. Everybody, including the royalty stood attentively and nervously waiting to hear the message of the Holy Man.

Throughout history the Maya High Priest had almost never been wrong in translating their visions in the outcome of wars, predicting eclipses, and other astrological revelations. "let your heart be at peace," The Holy Man added, "for today I bring only good news to you. We know for a certainty that the enemy of the Allied Cities, Red Cloud, is now dead, sacrificed by the very same people who vowed to help him overthrow his nephew in Chac'temal. The gods are smiling with us. Five peace emissaries from the Far North have arrived in Chac'temal with a proclamation of peace from their rulers. They respect our alliances and fear our great armies. They want peace."

Everybody gathered in the plaza, began jumping and dancing in happiness with the notion that their brothers, uncles, cousins and even fathers will not be risking their lives by engaging in battle after all. "At this moment, as we speak all armies are marching back to their respectable Cities."

"Only a few platoons will stay a few more days in a military outpost beyond Chac'temal. In another note," he continued, "one of the men that were missing after being attacked by Nohoch Pek and his men has been found. He is Box Balam of the Clouds Window's Clan, at this time he recuperating in Holpatin and he may soon join us." As the High Priest raised his right hand the signal for the people to go back to their jobs or home, everybody fell on one knee and placed their right hands across their chest slightly bowing their heads showing their respect and love to their Holy Men before leaving the Sacred Plaza.

The High Priest had once more correctly translated his vision from the gods protecting them from war. Once more the people of Lamanai proved that their High Priest was indeed the holiest of all High Priests from all the Maya Provinces.

The ambassador and emissary of Copan had been summoned to the Royal Court so Lord Nohoch Zak Mai could hear their plea. After hearing the message of the Ruler of Copan, Lord Nohoch Zak Mai decided that immediately a contingent of skilled farmers and soldiers along with corn, beans, fruits, vegetables and most importantly seeds to be dispatched to the city of Copan. His soldiers were ordered that they themselves supervise the distribution of the food and seeds to the people and farmers. He also declined the rulers offer in sending men to work in his fields. He had only one written message for the ambassador to take to his ruler and it was. "**Be fair and be just and most importantly love and cherish your people, for in this way, the people will love you back and the Gods will smile upon you, your city, and your provinces**."

A special invitation was also extended to the Royal Family of the city of Copan and all the Allied Cities to attend a very special ceremony to be celebrated in forty days, where a Sacred Game of Pok A Tok would also be played to honor and give thanks to the gods for sparing them from a dreadful war.

For two weeks Box Balam had lain in his hut healing. Seen to, by the medicine woman of Lamanai and assisted by Ixchel Quetzal, Ek Balam and Lady Tzuk, his mother. Some nights he would still wake up in the middle of the night screaming and sweating profusely. The savage encounter with Nohoch Pek his warriors and the ordeal he had to endure while being lost and injured in the jungle, was still fresh in his mind. The demons of Xibalba still tormented his soul and mind.

Worst of all the nightmares were not the open jawed snakes showing their long fangs, but the hairy botfly larvae living inside his skin and the leeches feeding in places where he couldn't reach them. Ten botfly larvae had been extracted out of his body by the medicine woman of Holpatin. Three of them had been buried deep in his scalp and the rest in his back and buttocks. At night it was as if he could almost still feel them feeding. It was as if his body was being stabbed with a sharp pointed Obsidian knife. The medicine woman had explained to him that it was mosquitoes that had deposited the eggs of the botfly in his body and not the botfly itself.

The botfly, she had said, would normally glue its eggs to the feet of a mosquito. It knew somehow that the mosquito had to puncture a hole in the skin of a mammal in order to feed on its blood, humans included. So it relied on the mosquitoes for its young ones to hatch. The warmth of a body allowed the Botfly eggs to immediately hatch then the larvae would burrow itself into the skin of the mammal and that would be its living host. If not extracted immediately the larvae can grow up to two inches in length inside its host. It was extremely painful when it fed. But, the old lady had said that because the larvae secreted a natural antibiotic, so its living food doesn't spoil; the hole it inflicted on its host skin doesn't gets infected. If not extracted before and after it becomes an adult it crawls out of its host fall to the ground, pupates, and then turns into a Botfly once more. Thus begins another cycle of life.

He remembered well how his brother and uncle had always searched their dog's skin thoroughly for signs of Botfly larvae after returning from a hunting trip. He didn't know all this medicine woman had told him, but he had seen the larvae being extracted from the skin of the dogs. They had used the same method as the medicine woman, a paste made from the tobacco leaf that was applied where the larvae was living and feeding.

"Not to worry," the medicine woman had told him, "eventually the nightmares will disappear, but for now it helps in taking out all the tension and fear you have inside you so the nightmares are normal and many times good." At the beginning of the third week after being brought back to Lamanai, early one morning and feeling much better Box decided to take a walk by himself towards his clan's artificial pond. As he got some water from the pond in a gourd to wash his face he remembered the movement he saw and the strange feeling he had had in the morning of his *Luum Mak* many weeks ago. He knew now that what he saw and felt that morning were the presence of the same people that had killed his friends. They were at that time looking for an opportunity to kill his uncle Crocodile Tooth.

He was very sad in having lost his friends but content that all this was now in the past. There were no more rumors or threats of war. The people of Lamanai and some of the Allied Cities were now living a normal life and now he would look at his future positively. Today he was going to ask Ixchel to be his girlfriend; His sister Ek had told him that Ixchel liked him a lot and he was not about to lose the opportunity in losing her to another boy. So his mind was made up and he would do it today.

While washing up, Box couldn't help thinking about his future and the future of his beloved Lamanai. In a very short time he had experienced the hardships of being an adult. He now understood why soldiers were always guarding the borders of the Lamanai Provinces.

Robbers, assassins, and even spies would always try to rob or kill an unsuspecting victim and worse of all they can be people that you once trusted. The crude reality of people in the brink of starvation in nearby Copan was difficult to fathom. Could this be Lamanai in the near future he asked himself, He had heard that like Lamanai, Copan was once a wealthy city and that its people always had more than enough to eat. Not anymore though, now he heard that people were moving away from there, looking for a better life, more to the North. Some peasants from Copan had even arrived in Lamanai seeking refuge. Years ago he had heard his father and uncle talking about Maya Cities beyond Caracol. About selfish and greedy rulers who always demanded more taxes from their people especially from the peasants.

The taxes imposed on these people, by their rulers, were huge and when they couldn't pay they would force them to work on huge buildings being erected for their conveniences. This created discontent amongst the population and this created huge migrations away from these cities. On some of his missions Crocodile Tooth and most recently, even Big Tapir had seen people with their families and their few possessions coming from Piedras Negras looking for a better place to settle and have a better life.

Just the week before, a group of five families coming from a western city beyond Tikal, had requested permission from Nohoch Zak Mai to form their own village in one of the provinces of Lamanai. Many of them were inexperienced farmers only using the slash and burn system of farming called *milpa* all of their life; But they had expressed their desire in wanting to learn from the skilled farmers of Lamanai in the raised fields method and other techniques. Box had heard that the ruler had adopted them into Lamanai and they were now being trained in the terracing agriculture techniques on hills, the ridged field system on the fertile rich swamps, the cultivation of Cacao, and other agricultural techniques.

The lack of farmland, Big Tapir, had explained were driving these poor peasants away from their cities. The rulers, in order to build these huge temples to be used as royal tombs for themselves and their families, required a lot of white lime to make plaster and mortar for the buildings. Limestone had to be burned at extremely high degrees of heat to produce white lime so this requires a lot of firewood from the forest. Huge tracts of forests had to be fallen in order to make firewood to burn the limestone. He also said that the people of Lamanai were always careful about this.

The rain forest only had a thin layer of black soil and if not protected it can be washed away by the rains and render the area useless for farming. This was what was happening in areas where huge tracts of forests were completely cleared. So, gradually the peasant farmers of the West were forced farther and farther away from their city to be able to grow enough food for their families. Moreover the excessive *milpa* system, slash and burn, used by these people and not giving the land enough time to fallow and recover its natural fertility were creating great damage to the forests. Huge useless savannahs were now growing around these cities, Big Tapir had explained to his younger brother, Box.

The howling of a big alpha male Howler Monkey on one of the tree tops, reminding the other males of his troop who was boss, brought Box back to reality. As Box Balam walked back towards his house he looked around and could see the prosperity of his beautiful city, yet, he still wondered. There were bigger cities to the far West and South of Lamanai that had been as wealthy as and maybe even more prosperous than Lamanai yet they were slowly going on a decline. Is this the way Lamanai is headed, he thought, is it possible that in short generations from now these great cities including Lamanai will be no more?

Lamanai also practiced the milpa system, they also used a lot of firewood to make white lime for construction, and they also engaged in wars, they also had to lay their farm land fallow.

As Box walked toward his house and climbed over a small hill, he looked at a huge majestic Rain tree growing about fifty feet away from the lagoon. Not too far away, a huge Ramon tree, a flowering Bukut and a great Mahogany tree was growing nearby too. But the Raintree was his favorite. It had always captivated his imagination; it was host to many different species of flowering epiphytes. Colorful bromeliads and beautiful exotic flowering orchids and tillandsias making their home on the tree, gave it a special beauty and it had been the inspiration for painters and artists from around the region for ages.

One particular flower that wasn't there before attracted Box's attention, it was growing on a limb at the very top of the tree almost hidden from sight. It was the wonderful Black Orchid flower, the favorite flower of the Princess and the Queen. The princess had actually been the one to first begin calling it, the Black Orchid—no one knew why since it wasn't black at all—. It had beautiful shiny dark purple petals with a bright yellow spot at the base and it was the most beautiful flower Box had ever seen. "As beautiful and delicate looking as Ixchel," He said softly to himself. At first he thought about climbing the tree and bringing it down for Ixchel; But then he thought that it would certainly be more romantic to bring her here to see it herself at the same asking her to be his girlfriend.

Looking at the beautiful tree and seeing for the first time a Black Orchid grow on it helped Box forget about the troubles of other cities. Looking beyond the trees Box could see the sparkling waters of the great Dzuluinicob Lagoon and on the East banks across the lagoon he could also see farmers hard at work tending their raised or ridged fields filled with all sorts of vegetables. The swampy areas on the Eastside of the lagoon were the most fertile of all other agricultural areas. A long low wooden wall had been built around the raised fields to protect the farmers from the many crocodiles that could be found in the lagoon. The crocodiles were sacred for the people of Lamanai, so they could never harm them; moreover they had named their city in honor of them hundreds of years ago.

"Our Ruler and High Priest are smart," thought Box, "they will never allow Lamanai to go on the way of other Maya Cities. The High Priest always pays his due respect to our gods and the Ruler has always treated his people kindly, fairly and with respect. Everybody agreed that Lord Nohoch Zak Mai loved his people very much. Moreover, the designated date of the celebration was fast approaching and another prisoner of war will be sacrificed to the gods and this will bring more prosperity to Lamanai," Thought Box. He was so deep in his thoughts that he did not hear Ixchel Quetzal sneak silently behind him and was startled by her touch on his shoulder. Ixchel had a radiant smile on her face and had been looking at Box for some time now.

He was so surprised that for a moment he was speechless. "I've been observing you for some time now," Ixchel said, "you were so deep in thought I didn't want to disturb you. What were you thinking Box?" Still surprised, he just pointed at the Black Orchid flower almost hidden behind other air plants and simply said, "My darling Ixchel you are as beautiful as that Black Orchid flower, the most beautiful flower growing on that tree. I love you Ixchel. Would you be my girlfriend?" She looked into Box's sincere eyes and kissing him with anxious red lips and sparkling eyes like the waters of the Dzuluinicob lagoon she said, "yes, yes I love you too Box."

Every afternoon he would come back to the Rain tree to admire it and the beautiful bromeliads and orchids growing on it. He would then sit on the hill top and look at the beautiful lagoon. Many times he would see children splashing and swimming in the enclosed area of the lagoon designated for swimming. The enclosed beaches were to keep away the crocodiles. He would sadly remember his best friend Red Cat and the times they had also gone swimming. Leaves of the Rain tree fell on top of him as the breeze swayed its branches to and fro. He smiled softly as he remembered the mischief he and Red Cat were always involved in when they were little boys. He could almost hear his voice as he reminisced.

"Box, Box," he could hear his friend Red Cat calling from outside his house. It was a grey overcast day and it had been raining heavily all night and it had just stopped an hour ago. Only a slight drizzle was falling. Box was lying on his hammock just listening to the birds that came every day to feed on the fruit trees near his house specially the Custard Apple tree. The children of his clan and others were not required to attend classes today since more rain was expected. Box and Red Cat had been ten years old at the time.

"I am inside Red," he shouted lazily still not getting up.

Red ran excitedly into Box's house and into his bedroom. His younger brother was not there, he had already gone to the kitchen to wait for his breakfast.

"Remember old man Cantuk? Well, he died last night, my mom just told me. At this moment they are arranging for his burial," said Red Cat excitedly.

This certainly aroused Box's curiosity so he jumped off his hammock looked at Box and eyed him suspiciously.

"Don't be telling me a lie or be tricking me just to get up, Red, because I won't forgive you this time."

"It is true boy, why would I tell you a lie?"

"Why!why? Because I know you Red that is why," Box snapped.

"It's true, go see for yourself if you don't believe," retorted Red, feigning being offended.

Box stayed a while more on his hammock looking at Red then finally said, "okay then, let's go see if it is true," still not totally believing.

Old man Cantuk was a popular old man who loved to get drunk on Balche wine. Almost every day he could be seen walking the streets of the city with a huge gourd of wine in his hands. When asked what he did for a living he would proudly say, I am a farmer and honey bee keeper," but in reality he was, officially, none of the above. He would earn his living by doing odd jobs for the people that had taken him onto their clan. Many times he did show up with gourds of honey from the stingless bee for sale, but nobody knew where he kept them.

Nobody knew where old man Cantuk came from or if that was his real name. People really didn't care for he was a gentle old man always telling jokes and stories to the children and he bothered or harmed no one.

It was rumored that he once was a strong, young, handsome and talented bee-keeper from the city of Uaxactun, but then, a terrible tragedy had befallen his family and that he had abandoned his city and wealth to go live as far away from his city as he possibly could in order to forget. Another version of the rumor on why he became a vagrant and a drunk was that when he was a young man, the feared evil creature of the forest the Xtabai had lured him with her beauty and tried to kill him but he somewhat miraculously escaped from her domains. It is believed, even though it never came from the mouth of Cantuk, that the evil Xtabai had casted a spell on him. That he would never marry and have a family and that he would be a vagrant and a drunk until he died.

The most credible version in why he became like this had been mentioned by the elder who had accepted him into his clan many years ago. He had said that Cantuk was actually once a hard working and dedicated bee-keeper from his native Uaxactun. The story goes that one day renegades had attacked his small village and had murdered his wife and two boys. His eldest daughter had also disappeared. The people believed that she had been kidnapped to be sold to the high priests of The North City who sacrificed young virgins to their blood thirsty gods. Cantuk had been in the City of Xunantunich with a contingent of merchants at the time.

It is said that when he got the news that his entire family had been murdered he became very distressed and went into a trance like state. After that he was never the same, he began drinking Balche wine excessively; he abandoned his bees and village and would walk the streets of the city and villages crying for his family. The people felt sorry for him so they gave him clothes and food every time he came around. He suddenly disappeared one day from his village and everybody gave him up as being dead. Five years later his relatives from Uaxactun found out that he was living in Caracol and after that Lamanai.

He no longer cried on the streets, in fact he seemed jovial and happy specially when drinking but he never spoke about why he had abandoned his village, his bees and all his possessions, for he had been rapidly becoming a wealthy young man. He told the story only once before many, many years ago and that was to the elder from Lamanai that had adopted him onto his clan and that had died ten years ago.

Red Cat ran towards the end of the plaza where Cantuk's dilapidated house was located, with Box following close behind. A group of people were already gathered in front of the house and a Chilam was already leading the gathered people in prayers.

"See, I wasn't lying," Red said to Box pointing his finger at him.

"Okay, okay," answered Box at the same time trying to get between the crowds so he could take a look at the dead old man.

"I know where he keeps his bees and honey," Red whispered in Box's ear.

This made Box jump a little and very surprised he asked, "what did you say Red?"

Many times the kind and friendly Cantuk would sit by the birds display at the zoo drinking and handing children pieces of honeycomb laden with golden sweet honey. The children of Lamanai loved him for this. All the children including little Red and Box would seek him out and beg him for the sweet delicious treat. Even the caged birds at the zoo seemed to get excited when they saw old man Cantuk approach their cages. For he always walked around with a pouch of ground maize that he used for feeding the birds. Occasionally, he would throw a piece of honeycomb inside the cages and the birds would excitedly start squawking and noisily fight for it. Old man Cantuk could have made a lot of money selling his honey but he only sold only enough to purchase his wine. Sometimes he would simply trade honey for good wine. He probably could have made the wine himself but making wine took a long time, so he didn't. After gathering his honey he would first present a gourd full of the precious liquid to the Royal Family then he would distribute the rest amongst friends and children.

After hearing his friend say that he knew where the dead Cantuk kept his stingless bees and honey, Box immediately lost interest in wanting to see the dead old man and he decided he wanted to see his beehives better. It was hard to believe, for no one knew where he kept his logs of bees. Other bee-keepers kept their bees inside a hollowed log sealed with mud on one end, near their homes in order to protect them from predators like the Red Eye frogs, Basilisks and other creatures, but not Cantuk and nobody seemed to know, especially not the children. In reality many grownups knew but they preferred that children didn't know. Everybody respected the kind old man's efforts in having a well hidden honey farm. Unguarded honey-bee logs filled with delicious honey were too tempting for young adventurous children.

"I heard my father telling my mom that Cantuk kept his bees by the Gray Fox pond about two miles from here," Red was excitedly saying.

Both little boys knew where the pond was located for they had gone fishing there many times but they had never seen anything slightly resembling a beehive and they had never seen Cantuk around there either.

"It is because he keeps it in the small island by the swampy area of the pond," Little Red was explaining to Box. At least that is what he thought his father told his mom.

"We have to go check it out Red," Box said with gleaming eyes.

"No, we can't, we will get into trouble. I also heard my dad say that after nine days his possessions would be given to the High Priest Lord Sac Pek. If anybody finds out we went there we can be in serious trouble."

"Come on Red, nobody will know, tomorrow morning we will tell our parents that we will go fishing and then we can take a look at the bees. We won't take any honey Red, promise, so we won't be in trouble."

Red looked at his best friend with suspicious eyes and said, "Okay, but if you take even a small piece of the honeycomb I will deny ever being with you."

The drizzle had stopped and the sky was clearing by the time the two boys decided to head home to have breakfast and to do their chores. They could not play ball this day or tomorrow for the field was very muddy and the ball wouldn't bounce on the mud.

Early the next morning Box was in front of Red's house calling for him. He had a long stick with a sharp point that he used for fishing. Armed with fishing gear and lunch the two boys headed happily towards the pond and Cantuk's delicious honey.

As soon as the young boys got to the pond they decided to immediately paddle to the small island. They found the small dugout canoe that someone had left there for some time and the same one they always used when they had gone fishing. They had never gone all the way to the island since they had always been cautioned about a vicious huge male crocodile that had its territory there. They had never seen it but they were very much afraid and they were smart enough to stay away from it. Now, they knew that the story about a huge vicious crocodile in the island was fabricated. It was done only to keep children away from the island and old man Cantuk's honey. When the two friends got to the island they, very cautiously and silently began searching for the bee hives. They were very careful, so as not to disturb the crocodile if in case the story was true and it was around. Then they saw it. About ten hollowed logs were set on top of flat rocks and bees were buzzing over it. The boys immediately knew that this was old man Cantuk's bees. The logs were completely enclosed by a net weaved so tightly together that only the bees could go through them.

"See that, Box. That is why he could keep his bees far from the city, the frogs and lizards could never get through those nets to the bees."

"He probably came here almost every day to check on them too," added Box

Forgetting the promise not to take honey, the boys searched and found one of the logs filled with honeycombs loaded with honey. They had just begun savoring the golden liquid when they heard adult voices approaching them. They only had enough time to sneak out of the enclosed area and dash towards their canoe.

As they were paddling rapidly away they recognized the canoes the men had used, they were canoes belonging to the Royal Guards. The boys were so frightened that after the boys parked the canoe they grabbed their fishing sticks and lunches and ran as fast as their legs could carry them back to their homes.

Box Balam continued looking towards the lagoon and at the kids laughing and splashing water at each other. "How many wonderful adventures we had together Red Cat my beloved friend," he whispered silently to the wind. "I shall never forget you Red."

He remembered that after they got home that day after visiting Cantuk's Island, as it was now called, they didn't come out to play for days. They worried that one of the guards may have seen them and that they would tell their parents. They would have surely been severely punished.

Later that week they laughed and joked about their little adventure. Each one teasing each other that he was running as if he had seen the spirit of Cantuk himself. In one thing they agreed and that was, that they were lucky that the guards had approached the small island from the opposite side they had. Nine days after that, they had seen Cantuk's logs and bees being brought to the Sacred Temple. On the tenth day they were distributed amongst the bee-keepers of Lamanai

Box Balam continued smiling as he got up and said a small prayer for the soul of Red Cat. He then admired the beautiful Rain tree filled with bromeliads and orchids once more, then made his way towards his home.

CHAPTER SEVENTEEN

For two weeks the people had been preparing for the great celebrations that would be held to honor the gods for sparing them from having to go to war. Huge ramadas (thatched shelters) had been built surrounding the Ceremonial Plaza where a special ceremony would be held to honor the late captain Chacbe, Red Cat and the other fallen sons of Altun Ha. There were also rumours that Box would be presented with an honorary shield for his heroic survival.

Near the lagoon was an open court yard that had been used as a marketplace for hundreds of years by the local farmers and merchants but for this special occasion it was designated to be used also by the visiting merchants of far and near. Every kind of grain, vegetables, fruits and cooked food would be on sale there. Polychrome vases, plates, pots, and all kind of effigies and statues made from clay, Jade and precious stones would be available for trade. Five hundred merchants would be coming from everywhere to display their goods for trade; they would also be bringing armors and newly invented weapons to display along with textiles, furs, skins, feathers and dyes.

This would be the biggest celebration the Allied Territories had ever seen. Every one of their cities would be sending delegates of Royalty, Ambassadors, Royal Guards and their entourage to witness the ceremony and the game of Pok-A-Tok. They would also be bringing along painters, sculptors and scribes to record this historical event on paper, wood, and stone.

Families of all the clans of Lamanai were preparing rooms and building new ones to host all the visitors on that day. For, after the ceremony the celebration would go on for three days. Ambassadorial residential complexes had been well prepared to host visiting dignitaries. A musical orchestra would be coming all the way from Tikal to join the ones from Holpatin and Lamanai; they will also be displaying and playing recently invented musical instruments as well as old ones. Itinerant performers would also be arriving in Lamanai for the festivities.

When the historic day finally arrived, thirty soldiers of the Royal Jaguar Order, the personal Royal Guards of the ruler of Lamanai, were standing at attention in three lines of ten in the middle of the Sacred Plaza. As soon as the Great Conch Shell horn at the top of the temple was blown, Lord Nohoch Zak Mai, his High Priest and the representatives of other cities started descending the palace steps toward the throngs of people that had gathered to witness the greatest ceremony in the history of the Maya People. On the west side of plaza were the twenty three young men who had recently celebrated their Luum Mak. On the spot where Red Cat should have been, was occupied by a tall carved

Stella depicting Chacbe, Red Cat, and Box Balam engaged in battle against evil forces.

Every one of the boys standing, including Box, had a beautiful red feather from the Scarlet Macaw in a band holding down their long black hair around their heads. The reward bestowed on them for having successfully accomplished their mission. Red Cats one had been presented to his mother. Box, was also presented with a special wooden shield depicting the emblem glyph of Lamanai for his heroic battle against Nohoch Pek. Every one of the boys was wearing the long tunic that had been presented to them on the day of their Luum Mak.

On their feet they wore sandals made from Tapir hide covered with jaguar skin and a long string securing it to their feet was tied around their ankles. At this ceremony the young men were presented with their very own war armor also made from Tapirs hide and cotton. New weapons were issued to them and every one of them was appointed to a profession he would be practicing. Box Balam, as excited as he was, didn't move a muscle as the ruler declared that he and seven other of his colleagues would be initiated into the Jaguar Order of Soldiers and their training should begin tomorrow. Lord Nohoch Zak Mai had made no mention of who was to participate in the Pok-A-Tok game the next day.

He was seated in the balcony of the palace with his wife on his right and Shining Blue Star, the beautiful princess, on his left. The mystical sounds of the musical instruments playing echoed across the Sacred Plaza and beyond. The beauty of this sacred sound penetrated the very soul of everyone who could hear it. The Royal Family and the Holy Men were seated just above the orchestra playing and the soothing tapestry of musical sounds gently lifted them in a state of pure awareness. The high priest and his acolytes were actually seated on a balcony below theirs. Everywhere surrounding the magnificent palace were members of the Royal Guards dressed in their ceremonial dress and fully armed.

The young princess smiled happily as she witnessed her people celebrating and dancing below in the Royal Plaza. As young and as innocent as she was, she understood that today could have easily been a day of lamenting and not celebrating. She had seen her city preparing for war and she had seen the distress on her father's face for many weeks. She had also seen the sad faces of the families that were bidding farewell to their young sons as they prepared to march towards Chac'temal to war against the forces of the Far North not knowing if they would ever come back alive. She stood and leaned against the low wall of the balcony and waved at the people celebrating below.

She loved her people dearly and vowed that if she became queen someday she would protect them as much as she possibly could. Like her "uncle" the high priest she hated war and she longed to see all the neighboring cities living in peace.

When the soldiers and the young men were dismissed, Box could hardly acknowledge the congratulations from his family, friends and fiancée Ixchel. His disappointment was huge in not being selected to play with the Royal Team so, faking tiredness, he decided to skip the celebration and go home accompanied only by his beloved Ixchel.

After an hour of being alone with Ixchel in his house he heard a knock in his front entrance. The High Priest, his father, his brother Big Tapir the present war chief, his uncle Crocodile Tooth the retired war chief and six other elderly men he didn't know entered his house. After instructing

Ixchel Quetzal to return to the festivities the High Priest said to Box Balam,

"I saw the disappointment in your face when our ruler didn't appoint you to the ball team Box, but that was not for him to decide." His father then surprised him by saying, "a committee is who decides which soldier becomes a member of the Royal Team of Pok-A-Tok, this group here is the committee of whom I have been a member for twenty years. So is your uncle. Your brother became a member automatically when he was appointed war chief." He held Box by the shoulders and continued saying, "of course, at first I didn't want you to be a Royal Ball Player. It is very dangerous and risky when you play in Ceremonial Games but I think that now you know that. When Big Tapir became a soldier I voted against he becoming one. I must tell you, though, that with you it's different. Everybody has convinced me that you would become a great ball player and that you would be an asset for the Royal Team." The High Priest, Sac Pek, then said, "We hereby declare you a new member of the Royal Pok-A-Tok team of Lamanai."

The next day inside the sweathouse beside the Sacred Ball Court, waiting for the horn to blow, that would announce the beginning of the Sacred Ball Game, stood Box Balam proudly with a smile on his face that was painted black and red. A huge Jaguar had been tattooed on his right arm as per tradition done to all new members of the Royal Team of Pok-A-Tok of the Great Maya City of Lamanai by the Great Dzuluinicob Lagoon. It was two p.m. Friday the twenty-second of August in the year six hundred and fifty one A.D. The temperature was at a pleasant eighty-four degrees Fahrenheit and the humidity was seventy-two percent and a refreshing South Easterly wind was blowing from the Lagoon. It was indeed a perfect day in the city of Lamanai. Everywhere, the players could hear the people chanting and cheering loudly and happily waiting for the game to begin and to see their beloved team. The great Conch Shell Horn then sounded and the eleven men of Box's team, wearing Jaguar skin uniforms, padded clothing, a wooden yolk around their waist, heavily cotton padded ankles, shoulders, elbows and a leather helmet on their heads, and Box Balam as their co-captain, ran outside the ball court to meet their worthy opponents.

Far away, on the branch of a young Mahogany tree, on top of a steep hill, unseen by humans, stood the magnificent, majestic, well fed, lean and beautiful five feet eight inches long, two hundred and seventy-two pounds female Jaguar overlooking the wonderful and beautiful city of Lamanai by the great Dzuluinicob Lagoon. She had just come from the river for she loved splashing and swimming in the water. During the day she rested and played with her young ones while at night she hunted.

Her ears were pricked forward. She could hear the music coming from the city beyond. She was alert and curious, yet cautious. She also saw with awe and interest at all the people dancing and celebrating in the city. Below her, at the bottom of the tree were two robust, healthy, happy cubs, a male and a female, playing roughly with one other. Every now and then, the mother Jaguar above, would growl an affectionate warning to them; to be cautious so as not to roll down the hill. She would actually be enjoying the company of her two cubs for several years before they ventured onto their own to seek their own territories As the wind slightly rocked her branch to and fro for a couple seconds, she looked upon the grandiose city such as a Ruler looks upon his or her kingdom, admiring it, some of them also hating it. She was also a Ruler, wasn't she? This was her domain; these awful humans had actually invaded *he*r territories. After all, wasn't she a Queen? Was not her mate a King? Were not they Rulers of the Rain Forest? There was even a temple built in their honor in the city below. "THE SACRED JAGUAR TEMPLE.

Far away, she could see the athletes playing Pok-A-Tok, and then she saw the unmistakable figure of Box Balam. He had a happy smile as he bounced a ball from his hip into a hoop. The mother Jaguar remembered him well. She knew that there was a special reason why the Peccaries were placed in front of her just as she was getting ready to devour the young boy weeks ago.

Throughout the days she was stalking him, she had seen how brave and determined he was in surviving, and she had respected him for this, but she was pregnant and hungry, so she had to try making him her meal but then the Peccaries appeared. There was no denying that the Gods were looking upon this young human who was named after them, Box Balam—Black Jaguar . . . .

Authors Note

A mere hundred and fifty years or so later, the alliance broke and the Maya sister cities began fighting one another. Foot soldiers ambushed and slaughtered complete Royal Families and established their leaders as rulers. Once sister cities, they were now fighting each other viciously for the rights to farmland and control over their realm, cities and people . . . . The Maya people never again lived in peace with one another.

HISTORICAL NOTE

THE SACRED BALL GAME ACCORDING TO THE
"POPOL VUH"
SACRED BOOK OF THE ONCE POWERFUL
QUICHE PEOPLE
"THE CREATION OF THE MAYA PEOPLE"

The Sacred Book of the ancient Maya, tells about the legend of twin brothers who were skilled in playing Pok-A-Tok. As they played, they made so much noise they disturbed the gods of Xibalba (Shibalba), who challenged them to a contest. The gods defeated the twins, sacrificed them, and buried their bodies under the ball court, except the head of one brother, Hun Hunapuh, which was hung on a tree of humanlike gourds. A curious young goddess named Xquic (shkwik) heard of the strange tree and decided to see it for herself. When she approached, Hun Hunapuh's head spat into her hand impregnating her with Hunapuh and Xbalanque (Shbalanke), the brothers known as the Hero Twins. In time these twins became even better players than their father and uncle. Summoning the brothers to a contest in Xibalba, the gods defeated them, ground up their bones, and threw them into a river. There the twins were reborn, first as fish then as itinerant performers.

Returning to Xibalba for revenge, they contrived an ingenious trap. After they demonstrated a variety of astonishing feats, Xbalanque beheaded Hunapuh—and then made him whole again. The gods were so delighted with this display that they begged to be sacrificed and then revived as well. The Twins appeared happy to oblige and began to dismember the gods. In the end they delivered the ultimate blow. By refusing to restore the gods to their original state, they defeated the dark lords once and for all. With good thus triumphing over evil, the Earth was now ready for the creation of human beings.

Xbalanque and Hunapuh emerged from Xibalba—the mouth of a cave, in the shape of a serpent—as the Sun and Moon, gifts to the Maya. Each day as these celestial bodies rise and set, the brothers re-enact their journey to the underworld and their joyful return.

In the way the ancient Maya saw the universe, caves are portals to the water-filled underworld, home of deities and a passageway to the Heavens.—Xibalba or "The place of frights"—It also plays a key role in the story of creation of the Maya People as described in the Popol Vuh the sacred book of the Maya.

HISTORICAL NOTE

THE DOWNFALL

By 900 A.D. most of the great Maya Cities had been completely abandoned, including Altun-Ha. Caracol, Copan and Tikal. Diseases, peasant uprisings, ecological failure, social upheavals, wars between sisters cities for more farmland, are only some of the contributing factors suggested by some of the Maya scholars. Everyday new discoveries are being made in the ruins of these once great cities. Today epigraphers are more and more being able to decipher the very complicated Ancient Maya hieroglyphs. Who knows, maybe someday we will get a revelation as to the real reason the Maya abandoned their great cities with some of their buildings still being under construction.

Lamanai in the other hand continued to thrive . . . .

AFTERWORD

LAMANAI

Lamanai adds up as the unbroken occupation in the Maya World. It not only spans all phases longest known of Ancient Maya Civililization, Pre-Classic, Classic and Post Classic Periods, but also tell a tale of ongoing Maya occupation and resistance for centuries after the Europeans arrived in the Americas. Lamanai was probably inhabited at least as early as early as 1500 B. C. up until about the eighteenth century. It was a major ceremonial center in Pre Classic times.

Lamanai probably was very important because of its location between the Caribbean Sea, the New River and its interior around 200 or 100 B.C. Its major buildings were constructed between then and 750 A. D. although additions and changes went up until at least the fifteenth century. Lamanai had at its peak a population of about 35,000.

By 1544 when the Spanish invaded Northern Belize they tried to set up a mission on the still thriving community of Lamanai but the Maya never readily accepted Spanish rule and a rebellion in 1640 left the Lamanai mission burned and deserted. Maya People continued to live here until the late 17th or 18th century when they were decimated by an epidemic, probably Small Pox.

Afterword

PRESENT DAY MAYA

Even though there are still many unanswered questions about the Ancient Maya Civilization. We know that they did not simply "vanish." We are still here today. The Maya People are today divided in different groups speaking related but differently understood dialects that presumably evolved from one common language. It is known that there may be over seven million Maya living in the Maya World today in Southern Mexico, Belize, Guatemala, Honduras and El Salvador. Kekchi, Mopan, Mam, Quiche, Cakchiquel, Chol, Chantal, Lacandon and Yucatec are some of the main Maya groups. The largest of the group, the Yucatec, over a million, live mostly in Campeche, Quintana Roo, and Yucatan in Mexico. Many of them also live in the North and West of Belize and I am a proud descendant of the Yucatec group from Northern Belize. On the South of Belize we have the Mopan and the Kekchi. Linguists believe that there may be twenty eight Mayan dialects—a couple of them extinct—divided into six sub groups Yucatecan, Huastecan, Tzeltatlan-Cholan, Kanjobalan, Mamean and Quichean.

The modern Mayan culture still carries some of their ancient traditions but many times, mixed with foreign traditions created by prolonged contact with outside influences. For example, Christianity and ancient Maya rituals is mixed with almost every activity including hunting, childbirth, and planting crop. Some of the same crops and agricultural methods used for thousands of years by their ancestors are still used today. In the South of Belize, modern Maya still sing chants, utter prayers, and make offertories to the same earth gods that gave care and protection to their plants and this is similar and typical of other Maya throughout the Maya world. In his book, RISE AND FALL OF MAYA CIVILIZATION, J. Eric Thompson, the English archaeologist and epigrapher, recorded a planting ritual he once observed in a Mopan Maya village in BELIZE.

The night before sowing, the helpers gather at the hut of the owner of the field. At one end of the hut the sacks of seed are laid on a table before a cross, and lighted candles are placed in front and to each side of a gourd containing cacao and ground maize. The seed is then censed with copal and then the hut, inside and out is completely censed. The men, who have brought their own hammocks, lounge in them, passing the night in conversation and music and the enjoyment of a meal served at midnight. Sometimes the group prays in the church for a good crop. The purpose of the vigil is to ensure that the crop will not be endangered by the incontinence of any member of the group [the Mam, the Chorti, the Kekchi, and other Maya groups observe continence for up to thirteen days at sowing time].

Looking back thirty years, I can see the group; most of them deep in shadow, for the guttering candles throw only a small circle of light. One or two are sitting in their hammocks; a third is lying back in his hammock with one foot dangling over the edge. Everyone is wrapped in a thin blanket, for the April night is cold and the chill air has no trouble in finding the spaces between the poles that form the hut. Conversation is soft, singsong Maya starts and dies like puffs of wind. Outside, the constellation of the tropics dawdle across the sky; they seem so close, one feels like raising his hand to push them on their course. Curiosity can hardly be delaying them; they have seen such vigils for many centuries. At day break the owner of the land goes to his field ahead of the rest of the party. There, in the center of his field, he burns copal and sows seven handfuls of maize in the form of a cross oriented to the four world directions, and recites this prayer.

O god, my grandfather, god of the hills, god of the valleys, holy god. I make to you my offering with all my soul. Be patient with me on what I am doing, my true God and [blessed] Virgin. It is needful that you give me fine, beautiful, all I am going to sow here where I have my work, my cornfield. Watch it for me, guard it for me, and let nothing happen to it from the time I sow until I harvest it.

ABOUT THE AUTHOR

MR. MANUEL M. NOVELO IS CURRENTLY A TOUR GUIDE IN THE BELIZE TOURISM INDUSTRY. HE SPECIALISES IN ANCIENT MAYA ARCHEOLOGY AND THE NATURAL HISTORY OF THE REGION.

MOST OF HIS STORY IS BASED IN AREAS SURROUNDING ORANGE WALK TOWN, BELIZE. WHERE HE WAS BORN AND RAISED. HE HAS WORKED FOR MANY YEARS IN THE TOURISM INDUSTRY OF HIS NATIVE BELIZE IN MAYA ARCHEOLOGY, CITY TOURS, NATURAL HISTORY TOURS AND CAVE EXPLORATIONS. HE IS A PROUD DESCENDANT OF THE YUCATEC LINGUISTIC GROUP OF THE MAYA PEOPLE.

HE CAN BE CONTACTED BY E-MAIL AT=== *belizemayatours@yahoo.com*

AUTHORS BIOGRAPHY

Manuel M. Novelo is currently a certified and licensed tour guide in the Belize Tourism Industry. He was born, raised and lives in Orange Walk Town, Belize. His area of expertise is in Ancient Maya Archeology Tours, Natural History of the region, and Spelunking. "The Sacred Maya Smoking Shell" is his first published novel. He is currently working on his second novel. He is a proud descendant of the Yucatec Linguistic group of the Maya People. He and his wife Elsy have three children Christy, Becky and Abner. They were all born in Orange Walk Town, Belize.